MOUTH

stories by
KERRY DONOGHUE

MOUTH
Copyright © 2025 Kerry Donoghue
All Rights Reserved.
Published by Unsolicited Press.
Printed in the United States of America.
First Edition.

No part of this book may be used or reproduced in any manner whatsoever without written permission except in the case of brief quotations embodied in critical articles or reviews. People, places, and notions in this book are from the author's imagination; any resemblance to real persons or events is purely coincidental.

Attention schools and businesses: for discounted copies on large orders, please contact the publisher directly.

For information contact:
Unsolicited Press
Portland, Oregon
www.unsolicitedpress.com
orders@unsolicitedpress.com
619-354-8005

Book Design: Kathryn Gerhardt
Editor: Summer Stewart
ISBN: 978-1-963115-31-4

BIG THANKS

This book is the product of love, obsession, the magic of a thousand small kindnesses, and one kidney stone. Got a lot of thanks to give.

Teachers are so often the first rainbows of hope. To my teachers, especially the late Ms. Ann Johnston. When you paid my entry fee to that high school writing contest, you took me seriously as a writer for the first time in my life. And that rewired the way I saw myself. To Kate Brady, Lewis Buzbee, and the incredible instructors at the University of San Francisco MFA in Writing Program, who listened and challenged and gave me the tools I still rely on. Teachers change our worlds. Pay them more.

To Amy, Sean, and Tim at Pistil Books from way back when in Seattle. Forever my favorite job and bookstore. You showed me more than just the ins and outs of bookselling (and how to make the most delicious vegan scones). Always buy indie.

To the readers and editors and literary staff who not only took the time to read earlier versions of these stories, but found something worthwhile in them. Your hard work gives the powerful gift of first chances. And extra love to Unsolicited Press, for giving me the chance I've always hoped for.

Also to Mrs. Ito, who saved all my handwritten horror stories from childhood. Please don't show anyone.

To my friends from down the street, and Camino and La Salle, the Seattle U crew, various speaker boxes, AHA, USF, ol' ESU, and beyond, oh how I cannot wait to celebrate with you ding dongs. You read the embarrassing poems I published in school newspapers, tolerated my super serious English major shoes, filled the audience at readings, and asked about my writing. You've always made it feel real, which has meant more than I can thank you for. Expect massive hugs and purple teeth very soon.

To Nurse Turbies, Goddess in the White Coat, thank you for fielding every horrible medical question I've ever thrown at you about infections, ointments, surgeries, and worst-case scenarios. Your thoughtful responses have been both frightening and illuminating and honestly, I'm going to keep texting you questions out of my own curiosity.

And to the staff at the old Rubio's in the Embarcadero, thank you for kindly clearing my plates every time I spread mahi mahi tacos and 3,000 versions of this manuscript on the corner table during the lunch rush.

To my family: from childhood, you imbued in us a love of storytelling. Whether it was with as many library books as we could carry or birthday tickets to *Phantom of the Opera* or that night we all went to the Pink Floyd concert, you made sure we saw lives bigger than our own. And you showed us that laughter will pull you through. I love you.

To Team Forever Stamps, Hannah Fairbanks and Pete Sheehy, my most trusted eyes. From autobio summer to nights in North Beach to teary-eyed video chats from my driveway, you've been there with hope and donuts. I am nothing without your eagle eyes and candor, your tracked changes, or your pep talks, and I feel endlessly lucky to journey this mad road with the two of you. This book wouldn't exist without your years of edits. You are the finest donuts in the case. Love your secret hearts forever.

Flynn and Luke, your stories have just begun. Go into the wild, beautiful world and find all the stories you can. And then fill your hearts, and the hearts of the ones you love, with only the very best words.

And to Scott. When I met you out on that kickball field with your hamburger sandwich, I thought I knew the meaning of love. How lucky I am to have been so wrong. Thank you for loving me at my best, my worst, and in every costume imaginable. You are all the words that matter.

ACKNOWLEDGMENTS

Earlier versions of these stories have been published in the following journals:

"A Step Ahead of the Alligator" was published in *The Pinch*, Issue 36.1, 2016.

"Birds of Paradise" was published in *The Louisville Review*, Issue 78, 2015.

"Casualties of the Vainglorious" was published in *Permafrost*, 41.2, 2020.

"Climate Change" was published in *Harpur Palate*, Volume 15, Number 1, 2015.

"Fever" was published in *The South Carolina Review*, Spring, 2016.

"Hunger" was published in *Painted Bride Quarterly*, Issue 96, 2017.

"You and Your Cold Soviet Heart" was published in *The Potomac Review*, Issue 56, 2015.

He couldn't bring himself to say it. That was me.
That was my dream. My dream just happened.
—Glen David Gold, *Sunnyside*

STORIES

Hunger	1
Fever	20
Casualties of the Vainglorious	39
The Ovation	64
A Step Ahead of the Alligator	80
Climate Change	100
You and Your Cold Soviet Heart	120
Birds of Paradise	139
Refrain	155
Jenny	178

MOUTH

HUNGER

Buick DeGaulle did not turn his head in time after he belched.

"Babe, please," Glory complained from the kitchen floor underneath him. After six months of marriage, she was almost immune to the stench of bratwurst and onions. But almost only counts in horseshoes, and now, with a child on the line, she was playing to win.

"Sorry," he panted. "Here I come."

Once he finished, Buick muscled out three quick push-ups, kissed her nose, and pulled out of her to grab some pretzels and pub cheese. Glory lay supine, willing her body to work like it should. When he returned to the floor with his snack, her legs were in the air, helping their unborn baby find the way home.

"What are you doing?"

"Stretching my back," she said.

Buick mopped his forehead. "I didn't hurt you, did I? You're getting so dang skinny."

"Thank you, honey." Truth was, she'd halved her daily calories during the last six months to prepare her body for a child. She ate only two meals a day now and one of those was a nonfat latte for breakfast. To keep her mouth busy, she'd snack on ice cubes, a trick that made her feel full without adding any extra calories. It was like cleaning the house for a new guest: the less she ate, the more inviting it would be for newcomers.

MOUTH

Glory remained on her back, curled on the sliver of linoleum in their kitchen. It was as dingy as the rest of their Milwaukee one-bedroom, but it was cheap, which was important now that they were trying for a baby. Well, technically only Glory had started trying; she just hadn't told Buick yet. Although they both wanted children, they could never agree on the timing. Buick insisted on health insurance, which his job at Radio Shack and hers at the salon didn't provide, while Glory craved the whole brood (plus a Christmas card with everyone grinning in dark jeans and white sweaters) right now.

During her weekly inspection on their honeymoon, she'd tweezed eleven wiry grays from her scalp, and it was as if all the clocks in her body had struck, a loud and public tolling. Her bridesmaids already had at least one child each; her maid of honor had three.

"Before we turn thirty," she'd pleaded with Buick when they returned. "We don't want to run out of chances."

Of course, he had never said that he was ready, but his brown eyes implied it, she knew them well enough. They hugged each other that night outside the bowling alley, just like they'd done most weekends during high school, swaying in the lake breeze, their bodies twined in a wordless pact that calmed the trembling depths of her being.

Buick dunked his pretzels and stared at the black gash where the doorknob bashed the wall whenever the front door opened. "We've got to patch that already. It's embarrassing." The hole gaped, a stale yawn into the drywall, their lives.

"I know." She began the Lamaze breaths she'd perfected—in through the nose, out through the mouth—to calm her excitement. Their baby could be inside her right now. She had to stay relaxed, so she imagined how she'd decorate the nursery: all mint and brown, a cozy woodland scene with two wide-eyed fawn decals sipping from a sparkling stream. The soothing came like a cool hand to the forehead.

Bringing her legs down, Glory clenched her pelvic muscles in quick sets to make sure her son—or daughter, but hopefully a son that they would name Harrison after her dead father—would get to where he needed to go. Harrison DeGaulle. It sounded better than blue-collar. At barbecues, the DeGaulle aunties were incorrigible when it came to Buick's name ("Because that's where you were made, baby boy"), and he'd vowed to give his own kid a better one.

"Thirsty?" he asked, hunching in front of the refrigerator.

"I'm parched."

He poured himself a glass of milk and then a glass of tap water for her. "I'm liking this frisky new you." After downing his milk in three gulps, he let out a satisfied sigh at the end.

Glory sipped her water, silently.

***

Later that morning at the fold-up card table they used as a dinette, Glory and Buick surveyed their piles. Masking tape divided the table into two heaps: to be paid and past due. They hoped that keeping their bills right out in the open would motivate them to make big bucks. Mostly, though, it made it harder for them to sleep.

Glory flipped through the receipts, tapping numbers into the calculator without even looking. Her bookkeeping skills were impeccable, which was one reason she knew she'd be a great mother. She also liked to organize, make lists, and map out each week's social plans on the calendar. She was at her best when she was in control.

"Think we'll make rent this month?" Buick asked while his cell phone buzzed.

"It'll be tight." Glory flinched while the buzzing continued. "Answer it already."

"Sterling!" Buick scurried into the bedroom to talk to his younger brother.

According to her calculations, they would have fifty-three dollars for the week after they paid rent, two Discover bills, the lease on their dented Kia, Buick's parking ticket, and the last of their wedding vendors. Glory smoothed her palms up and down her legs, her fingers sliding along the sharp shin line, noting the prickly parts where the Nair had missed. She snuck in a few leg lifts under the table to relax. Each movement burned one calorie that put her closer to her child. Soon enough, she'd find out if this month's efforts had paid off. Just the thought of baby powder gave her the energy to do twenty more lifts.

Buick ducked back into the kitchen. "Sterling's coming over for dinner."

"Do we have enough food?"

"He's blood, Glory."

She glared at him. "And we can't deny blood."

***

Sterling arrived at the apartment with automotive fanfare. Although Buick loomed at six-foot-four and had to duck under doorways, his younger brother was squat, which he made up for with a monster truck and steady diet of protein shakes. The truck was a rolling showcase of gold airbrushed flames and dashboard bobbleheads; tucked in the center console was a trove of lambskin condoms. "Extra large," he'd wink whenever he gave Glory and Buick a ride home from the bar. Sterling had worked day and night construction jobs to get his frame raised so he could feel above it all, or at least above traffic, even though he had to use a crate just to enter the cab.

"Come here often?" Sterling drawled as Buick opened the front door.

"Did two hours ago, if you know what I'm saying."

"Ten-four, good buddy!"

Glory closed her eyes. "I can hear everything, you know."

Sterling strode the three steps from the front door to the kitchen table. "Hey, sexy mama."

"You smell like skanks."

"You're not wrong."

As soon as he kissed the crown of her head, Glory panicked, worrying that he'd mussed the strategically placed strands covering her thin sections. She had lost some hair lately, catching stringy brown clumps that plunged like waterlogged mice when she was in the shower. And that was another reason they had to have a baby soon.

Sterling groaned. "You would not believe my night."

"You actually remember it this time?" she asked.

"Not really. But this helps." He pulled down his collar, exposing a purple cluster of hickeys.

Buick laughed and high-fived his brother. "So a second date at Planned Parenthood? Such a romantic."

"I'll pay for it. I can be a gentleman." Sterling snatched the foam cheesehead off their bookshelf and strutted like the Packers had just scored. Then he helped himself to the milk carton.

Catching knife-eyes from Glory, Buick slammed the fridge shut. "Sterling, save some for us, will you?"

She stormed toward the bathroom. "You guys are dipshits."

"You're hot when you're mad!" Sterling called.

Buick smacked his brother. "Don't make it worse," he whispered.

Shaking, Glory gripped the bathroom sink. She kept a bottle of baby shampoo in the shower as motivation, so she took several calming inhales of it. Once she was certain Buick and Sterling were busy cheering on motocross in the living room, she started her weekly inspection.

Her thighs had fluctuated over the years, leaving plum-colored claw marks along the curve of her hips as if her body was trying to escape itself. She took off her shirt. Then her pants. And then her bra, and once she was topless, she jiggled. What was the point of having this equipment if she wasn't going to use it? If they didn't act quickly, it would all go to waste. She sucked in, noting how her body dimpled in places other than her cheeks, too dented to love. She did four reps of calf-raises, four sets of wall-sits, and then she hooked her fingers onto the sides of her panties, tugging them to her ankles to find what else needed work. Glory paused.

Staining her underwear was the wrong answer to all her questions. She reached for the tampons.

***

Glory let Buick play with her hair in bed that evening. Midnight seeped through the skylight and when he noticed her crying, he cradled her, proving he wasn't afraid of tears, which would come in handy if they accidentally had a daughter. She let herself get scooped. Since she'd been more prone to the chills lately anyway, it felt good to nestle herself against his chest hair, to smell him and be so small.

"I know this is a tough time for you right now," he said.

She nodded. Six months of trying with nothing to show. Plus, she'd tweezed another nine gray hairs.

"We're working so hard for this and it's just not happening," he said. "But it will. We'll just work harder."

"Okay, baby." Glory liked when he became husbandy and powerful, another reason he'd be a good father. She pictured Harrison as a teenager sneaking out of the house, Buick reprimanding him with a stern voice and a firm hug. Forgiveness warmed her as she sunk into his brawn.

"I mean it," he said. "I'm really going to try. I want this."

"You do?"

"Yeah. I'm tired of penny-pinching and having holes in the apartment and not being able to bowl anymore. It's time for us to get serious. For me to step up and be a man."

It was as if he'd read and memorized the secret script inside her. "I'm so happy you say that, Buick. I didn't realize how much I wanted a baby until recently."

"Whoa, that's a whole other topic," he said. "Let's just focus on this first."

"Focus on what?"

"Money. I had a chat with Sterling while you were in the bathroom and it's time I put my best asset to work."

Glory stiffened.

"Nothing's working out like we thought it would," he said. "I can't find a job that makes me happy, and you aren't making much at the salon, so why waste more time? I decided to do what I'm good at and give competitive eating a real go. Not just stupid county fair shit. I'm going pro—for you and me and our future." He patted the firm barrel of his abdomen.

A chill flushed through her. "And you think that'll get us where we want to be?"

"Don't you trust me?"

"I do, Buick. But time's ticking." She imagined his body going soft, his focus going to the left of her. And more waiting.

"Don't worry," he said, kissing her. "Besides, there's no way this dump is ready for a baby."

She shuddered. "That's clear."

***

Sterling showed his support for Buick's new career by coming over every night to "talk strategy." He also ate all their food, hogged their cable, and inevitably wiped himself down with their last clean towel—so many extra costs that could've been avoided if he just chipped in forty-five dollars each month. But Buick wouldn't hear of it. Instead, he made a big deal of thanking Sterling for the frozen pizzas or gas station sandwiches he occasionally brought for dinner.

"You have to do it just like Kobayashi," Sterling said one night, showing Buick video clips of the Japanese champion. "That guy's a third your size and can eat your entire body weight in burgers. You're better off not chewing. Just swallow things whole."

Glory frowned in the kitchen. "Maybe he's not ready for that yet."

"Sure he is. Buick's a big boy."

So Buick started small with plain donut holes, dunking them in water before shoving them toward the dark horseshoe of his throat. Once he could control his gag reflex, he began training without water, and when he was comfortable swallowing unchewed pieces, he moved on to chicken wings. Because bones and hot sauce were involved, though, the wings were his biggest challenge, so he expanded his stomach to fighting size by loading up on shredded cabbage between sessions. "Gotta pound twelve thousand calories in each contest. Let's get this gut to the size of a football."

He practiced, his lips stretching unnaturally wider than his smile, his tongue wet, slopping. The stress of money and baby-making and being the perfect mother had stifled Glory's appetite, like someone had shoved a dry napkin down her throat. No more casseroles, or cheese curds, or even state fair cream puffs. No more nachos grande for lunch. And worse, no more Friday night fish fries. They couldn't afford these luxuries anyway, though the cravings would spike with such fury that she once considered using her bumper to nudge some distracted parishioners through the crosswalk so she could get her fudge-covered cookies before the Piggly Wiggly closed. To support her husband, Glory ate shredded cabbage dinners, too.

"That's not much, hon," Buick said one night before Sterling arrived. "Don't you want something more?"

She glanced at the way her tank top clung to her flat stomach. Then she looked at her watch: 6:51 p.m. She just knew she was ovulating and realized her intuition was yet another reason she'd make a good mom. Glory could sense when a rainstorm was coming and when the pork roast was done before the timer even buzzed.

"I do," she said. Hurrying to the couch, she started undressing.

"What? Now?"

"We're newlyweds, aren't we?"

"Can't I finish my dinner first?"

"We can do it standing, mix it up." Glory stripped off her pajama shorts, posing casually, as if all the trying-to-conceive Internet forums hadn't sworn that standing sex encouraged the boy sperm to hit their mark.

"I have a mouthful of cabbage. Maybe later?"

"How much longer am I supposed to wait, Buick?" Remembering she was topless, she sucked in her stomach.

His silence shouted.

"I just meant you haven't entered any contests yet," she said. Thankfully, she had on her good bra, so she angled her breasts toward him to salvage the moment. "Come on, baby. It'll ease your stress. Plus we can add the living room wall to our list of places we've done it."

Sighing, Buick plucked the cabbage strands from his lips and trudged to his wife.

As they bounced against their wedding portraits, she remembered the cellulite that must be rippling across her thighs. If he noticed the ugly stuff, he wouldn't want to touch her anymore. And then she wouldn't get pregnant, and then all her aunties and cousins and neighbors, who were perpetually six months and glowing, would secretly pity her as less than a woman, or worse, as That Woman Who Can't Have a Baby, Poor Thing. Glory lowered her hips to make the dimples less noticeable.

"Can't get a good grip on you," Buick said, squeezing her tighter.

She imagined his fingers disappearing into the pitted skin of her thighs until he was knuckle-deep in all her fat, Glory too disgusting to touch. Buick's body had turned doughy lately, but he still felt dense and strong, like a sack of rice. He could wear his extra weight as a medal of manhood—it was so easy for men. She wondered how many calories she'd burned.

Head back, his mouth slack, Buick was close to finishing. Glory liked to witness his climax because she wanted to remember his expression right at the moment they made their baby.

He pulled out. "I can't."

"Don't waste it." She used her fingers to shove his seed back into her then dropped to the floor so she could get her legs in the air. There had to be a little inside her. She rolled back even farther than usual, ensuring Harrison had plenty of opportunity to make himself comfortable.

"Waste what?"

"We were almost there."

"I wasn't. Jesus, you're getting so weird about stuff nowadays." He frowned at her contorted body. "And why do you keep doing that? Is your back still hurting?"

Staring into the gash by the door, Glory wondered how cold it was inside and if it reeked, damp and moldy. "A bit."

"You should get that checked out."

She nodded.

MOUTH

***

Sequestered in their bedroom that night, Glory flipped through chapters of *What to Expect When You're Expecting* while Buick and Sterling studied Joey Chestnut's eating technique and chugged beers in the living room. According to her monthly tally, they'd had intercourse nine times so far, seven of which had been missionary, just like all the baby books had promised was best for insemination. She'd been taking her prenatal vitamins, watching her weight. She googled male infertility.

After a good hour of research, she ripped off the sheets, fuming. Buick was deliberately sabotaging his sperm production by acting like an anaconda that had slithered into a backyard barbeque. But why would he go to such lengths to ruin all her plans? The question sent her back to the internet until she found a diagnosis that fit. Of course: he must be shooting blanks. She didn't need a doctor to tell her that. Besides, that's what mothers do–they diagnose. Flus, colds, aches, and itches. Wasn't every mom basically a country doctor? When Buick eventually stumbled to bed after midnight, she pretended to be asleep.

Between his snores, she could hear Sterling rifling through their fridge. She slid out of bed and, grabbing her ylang-ylang oil, dabbed some in her cleavage.

"Hey, sexy mama," Sterling slurred when she joined him at the table. "Did I wake you?"

"Yeah." She eyed the Tapatío scramble in front of him. "But it's okay. I'm hungry."

He pushed the plate toward her, his stink meaty, whiskey sweet. "Help yourself."

She took a bite. "You want a beer?"

"Hell yeah."

She grabbed two Pabsts and then they cheersed. Leaning back in her chair, she let her legs stretch between his.

"What's up?" He took a long sip from his beer, his blue eyes bloodshot. The sibling resemblance was most obvious in their faces, a fact that comforted Glory as she hurried through her beer. "Damn, does it smell like a Victorian funeral in here?"

"I need a favor," she said.

"Tell me."

The beer tasted bitter, but she drank quickly. "Something's off with Buick and I'm hoping you can fix it."

"I know you're pissy about his new job, but alls I can say is have some faith in the poor guy," he slurred.

"No, it's not that."

"What then? You're acting weird, even for you."

She dropped her voice. "I think Buick's broken."

"You're crazy. He's a machine. Haven't you seen how much he's been eating?"

Glory slugged her beer. "Broken in a different way." She rested her hand on Sterling's thigh. His leg felt narrower than Buick's, more muscular.

He squinted down at her fingers and then at her face. "Everything okay?"

"With your help, it will be." Taking his hand, she pulled him to standing, steadying him as he wobbled. She knew he was a butt guy so she let her hands drift, cupping his back pocket.

"What are you doing?" He knocked into the chair.

"Asking for a favor." She righted the chair, listening for Buick's drunken footfall.

"Stop it. That's so wrong, Glory."

"I know." She guided him through the living room and unlocked the front door. "Which is why we can't tell him. I don't want to embarrass him."

"About what?"

"He can't have kids, Sterling."

Pushing himself away from her, Sterling stumbled. "My brother? He never told me that."

"Like he'd ever ask for help?"

Sterling rubbed the back of his neck.

"Besides," she said, "haven't you secretly wanted to? With me?"

Flushed, Sterling looked away. "I can't do this to him."

"Then do it *for* him."

Glory reached out. He refused her eyes.

"Please? For Buick?"

Sterling took her hand.

"For Buick," she promised, leading him to the backseat of his truck.

***

Weeks passed. During that time, she'd picked up several shifts at the salon while the regular waxer had jury duty. Glory spent her days ripping hair from eyebrows, legs, undercarriages, each pull giving her a satisfying sense of accomplishment, order. It was a nice distraction from the impending round of pregnancy tests.

And an excuse to dodge Sterling, who'd been avoiding her like a summer-stuck delinquent.

When her period was officially three days late, she offered to do the grocery shopping, something Buick handled.

"You take a load off," she said. "I've got this."

"That's sweet, babe," Buick said, kissing her cheek. "Thanks."

As she hurried to the supermarket, Glory critiqued her reflection along the storefront windows. She tried to catch herself in natural poses, like when she was striding down the sidewalk or waiting for the light to change, to imagine how other women saw her. Her hip bones had started jutting out again, cute with the low-rise jeans she'd bought from the teen section at Kohl's. But even though she weighed the same as a high school junior, or maybe even a sophomore if she didn't eat anything salty, she was, in fact, almost past her peak baby-making years. She pictured baby Harrison coming out in a puff of dust.

With forty dollars to spend, she grabbed a roast beef hoagie for Buick, a loaf of white bread, a packet of string cheese, three Yoplaits, some kielbasa, and two cans of garbanzo beans. Then she beelined to the pharmacy section for a box of pregnancy tests. She'd been cleaning house for so long. She deserved a reward.

The supermarket had a single-stall women's bathroom with plenty of room to pace. She could also burn some anxiety doing tricep dips on the sink's ledge. Her hands shook while she sat on the toilet, activating the tests.

Someone knocked on the bathroom door. "Will it be much longer, ma'am?" an elderly woman yelled.

Ma'am. As if she looked like a woman who had a toddler. Glory grinned. "Going as fast as I can."

MOUTH

More than anything, Glory wanted to be a good mom, the kind with a hockey photo pinned to her purse, who would let the scouts camp overnight in the backyard, and maybe, when Harrison was older, drink alcohol. But only inside the house and only one hard cider. She imagined all the memories they'd put in picture frames from summers up north and Harrison's first ski lesson on the bunny hill. They'd be happy and giggling and the twenty-seven hours of labor that she'd been in, without an epidural because she wanted to prove she could do it, would be worthwhile.

Glory wadded her purse under her T-shirt, admiring her reflection in the mirror. On instinct, her left hand rested atop her protruding belly while her other hand curved underneath. The pose came so naturally to her. She knew what kind of pregnant she wanted to be: the cute kind, where her body stayed small and the baby was just a round ball that looked darling under maternity shirts. Strangers would want to rub her belly and she'd be absolutely luminous from all the attention.

The lady knocked harder.

With the test sticks in hand, Glory turned from the mirror and did one, two, three tricep dips, the calories just blowing away, far from her clean house that was all ready for a new guest. She added fifteen seconds to the suggested wait time, swallowed a deep, dry breath, and then peeked.

***

On the walk home, Glory felt perfect. She was a star: Jennifer, Julia, Meg. But even sunnier. Happier. Though she was tempted to skip all the way home, she wanted to take it easy and do everything right. Her hard work had paid off: Glory was bursting.

At the apartment, she noticed Sterling had shoved his monster truck into a compact parking spot, just like he'd probably shoved his ass onto their ratty couch. She grit her teeth. He couldn't have gone hunting this weekend? Maybe there was a Brewers game on at the pub? When she arrived at the apartment, however, their living room was jammed with construction workers.

No one noticed as she entered. At her height, she could only glance through the rowdy spaces between men, the air reeking of green peppers and armpits and nickels. In the living room, Buick sat facing two platters of orange-stained chicken wings.

"Buick?" She jostled her way to him. "Are you serious?"

"Hey babe! Surprise. Told you I had the answer."

Glory wanted to tell him that she did too, that it was tucked away and growing as they spoke, but he was tightening the bib around his neck.

"Who are all these idiots?"

"Mostly Sterling's friends from the worksite. Ready to see me unleash the beast?"

Her hand skimmed her belly. "I don't know. Should I go?"

"No, stay. Watch me."

The guys started chanting. Sterling, two inches taller than normal in his construction boots, slid into the chair next to Buick, avoiding her eyes.

As the chants gained speed, someone named Tony cupped his hands like a megaphone. "Food warriors to the table."

Buick and Sterling high-fived, her kitchen towels tied around their necks.

MOUTH

"Contestant number one is a force of his own. Part man, part machine, all stomach. He skids into this competition with the pedal to the metal. Let's welcome Buick DeGaulle to the table!"

The crowd hollered, launched a dirty paper towel at Buick.

"Contestant number two is stronger than the jaws of life. Welcome Sterling 'The Mouth' DeGaulle!"

Everyone booed. Sterling pouted and pretended to cry.

"Today, we eat with Picnic Style Rules. Winner gets three hundred bucks. Brothers, start your enzymes." Tony took a dramatic inhale. "On your mark, get set, eat!"

Through the crowd, Glory saw Buick grab each wing, dragging the bone along his front teeth, his tongue shoving the meat down the back of his throat. He'd been practicing that for weeks, his "chew-free" technique from the internet videos. Sterling ate the same way. Both men had orange fists and smeared cheeks.

"The Mouth is double-parked in first place at fifteen wings, with Buick chomping close behind at thirteen."

Glory hadn't eaten anything other than cabbage in three days. So many men crammed into the apartment. Her house. Her clean, neat house.

"It's wing-to-wing between brothers. The Mouth is at twenty-two, but Buick is snapping right along at twenty."

"Stoke up, bitch!" someone yelled.

Buick's face was red and straining, tears brimming.

"Push through those meat sweats! You're almost there," Tony barked.

Sterling mopped his forehead, glancing over at his brother. Glory could tell he was stalling to let Buick catch up. Then Sterling locked eyes with Glory. Unhinging his jaw, he let a deep belch slide out. She couldn't turn away in time, galvanizing her brother-in-law in a memory she knew she'd never forget.

Tony whooped. "You snooze, you lose, Sterling. Here comes Buick across the finish line!"

Glory stumbled into the kitchen. Mother, lover, doctor, provider. Mother, lover, doctor, provider. She was everything she'd ever wanted. A milk carton, half-opened, sat on the countertop. She stuck her nose inside, the stink sharper than she expected. Glory gagged with each inhale but couldn't stop, over and over, the stench as filling as the hope.

FEVER

Harlan savored each burning swig of gin as Jezalyn drifted into the muddy Tennessee. Between wispy riverbank weeds, mosquitoes cycloned around him. He slapped one dead on his neck, enjoying his slow afternoon buzz, the sun pulsing through the wilted dogwoods. While he stretched his legs, sweat rivered down the backs of his thighs into the dark valleys of his cutoffs. It was only noon and the heat already had a chokehold on the day. Harlan tore off the crust of his bologna sandwich and regarded his sister with his good eye.

Jezalyn adjusted her snorkel mask, setting her lips onto the breathing tube. Sludge suctioned around her feet, each slogging step a cadence that lulled Harlan closer to sleep. She swam farther out, a plastic grocery bag trailing in her hand, billowing into the ripples. Jezalyn dove under.

He timed his swill until she surfaced, waving something she'd found. Harlan wanted to wave back, to let her know he saw and was proud, but it was too hot to lift his arm. Too damn hot for anything. He didn't even want to strip off his tank top and ball it under his head. Harlan didn't know how she did it every day. She dove under again.

He closed his eyes.

***

"You done yet, Harlan?"

Twisting out of sleep, Harlan awoke to his neighbor Mason squinting down at him.

"I said have you fixed my machine?"

Drool crackled off Harlan's chin as he yawned and took in his surroundings. Evening had inked the sky. He jerked awake. "Where's Jezalyn?"

"Up at the house," Mason said.

"Thank god." His adrenaline eddied into a skull-cleaver.

"God got nothing to do with it. Jezalyn's just three years younger than you and a fine swimmer."

"I can't worry about my baby sister?"

"She's twenty-seven, Harlan." He nudged the paper bag at Harlan's feet. An empty gin bottle edged out. "Didn't finish what I paid you for, I gather."

The sky spun. Harlan anchored his feet and leaned his right hand on the ground. He shut his eyes, but it was worse that way so he focused on a rock. "Your washing machine'll be ready in the morning."

"If you weren't so damn good, I'd punch you, Harlan."

"That's what all the ladies say."

Mason sighed. "I'll swing by at eight."

Harlan tried to steady his hand to make the okay sign.

"Go help your sister," Mason said, shaking his head. He ambled down the banks back to his house.

Harlan rubbed his good eye. Hangovers were hard enough, but having only one sure eye made them even worse. When he was nine, Mason, Mama, and Jezalyn had moved in with Uncle Joel for the summer. Mama was usually too hungover to rinse their cereal bowls and, fed up with her cranky retort one Tuesday morning, Uncle Joel clocked the backtalk right out of her mouth. Harlan had grabbed a broom and whacked his uncle's knees, which only made the fist from Uncle Joel land even harder. Harlan knew how sorry Mama felt about his eye because she made chocolate chip pancakes every morning for a full week after. Harlan promised himself right then that he'd never hit a female and he'd held true to that his whole life.

When he entered the house he shared with his sister and her two Catahoula hounds, Jezalyn was crouched at the oven, smoking a cigarette and prodding a tuna casserole. "Back from the dead," she said. "My cooking smell that good, Harlan? Or you out of gin?"

"I was just napping, Jezz."

"Sure enough." She pulled the casserole from the oven while her hounds sniffed around her. "No matter. Pull up a seat."

"You smoking again?"

"No." She stubbed it out.

"I thought you gave that up for diving?"

"It's just one." Jezalyn scooped some casserole into the dog dish. After a few quick licks, the hounds' gray and white speckled faces glanced up at her again. She gave them both another scoop.

"Come on, Jezz, I'm hungry." Harlan stole a forkful from the dog dish, but Jezalyn slapped his hand.

"Could you do it proper for once?" She heaped a steaming serving onto his paper plate. "Don't need another dog in this house."

He eyed the hounds. "You find anything good out there today?"

She nodded at a digital watch on the counter. "Untangled that Casio from some eelgrass. Bet I can bring it back with a good buff and a new battery." As she pointed her spoon at him, an orange chunk of cheese fell to the table. "I'll be just as good as the Aussie divers, you wait."

Every day before her job as a polisher at the jewelry store, Jezalyn practiced diving, rising with the sun and then biking to the shore where she'd strip down to drag the river bottom. She could hold her breath for thirty-seven seconds, though traditional Japanese divers could hold theirs for two full minutes. She'd read all about it in the diving book she'd borrowed from the library three years ago and couldn't bear to return.

"I can hold so much now, Harlan."

He considered Jezalyn's petite frame and upturned nose. Her forearms and calves were toned from swimming, which their mother had taught Jezalyn in first grade when all Mama's bad luck had started. After Daddy had shoved a 12-gauge in his mouth to hush the voices in his head, a trail of men started visiting Mama's bedroom like ants to pie. Anytime one of them yelled or shattered a wine bottle, Jezalyn would hustle down to the river and inch on in, Mama running after her to yank her out until eventually she said, "Might as well learn how to get yourself out, missy." So she towed Jezalyn to where she couldn't stand and taught her how to dog-paddle.

Then Mama took to disappearing right after they got home from school. She put Harlan in charge each evening, which meant cinnamon sugar toast for dinner and late-night reruns of *Three's Company*. Mama would creep in at breakfast, the night still clinging to her like sweat-soured lilies. She kept it up until she died, when they found her keeled over in the neighbor's grass a block away, her purse full of bills, paid and ready to be mailed.

MOUTH

Harlan saw it for himself when he went to the morgue to ID her. He didn't tell Jezalyn she was gone until he finished an eight-shot pit stop at the bar.

Harlan blinked. With her blonde hair up in a scrunchie, Jezalyn looked just like their mother. Especially at the stove in their dead mother's house, one hand on her hip. But Mama had been cold for almost a year now. Harlan shook the thought from his head, touching the brown curls he got from their daddy. It'd been years since he'd been around, his face nothing more than a ketchup-stained Polaroid in their memory, so Harlan didn't know what he'd end up looking like and that scared him if he dwelled on it too much.

They took their plates to the kitchen table as usual, sitting in cold gray folding chairs at the heads of the table. An old Zenith rested on a stack of cookbooks.

"Something good coming up?" he asked between bites. The table wobbled. Or maybe he did. He sat up straighter.

"It's seven-thirty, Harlan." Jezalyn turned the volume knob until she heard the familiar voice reel, "Wheel of Fortune!" She clapped, scooting back to her chair, eyes locked on the screen.

"What're you waiting for, Jezalyn?" He scraped his plate.

"This," she whispered. "Stop ruining it."

Vanna White floated onto the screen in cobalt blue, sequined up, smiling and waving to the welcoming audience. In the middle of the stage, she swirled, the lights catching like fireflies on each gleaming spangle. With the dress cascading down her body, Vanna gazed into the spotlight as if it were just another perfect sunrise. She was posture, grace, strong white teeth.

"Every night, this one moment's all about her. Can you imagine?"

Harlan tried. "No."

Vanna tilted her head as if to personally welcome Jezalyn. A diamond cuff on her long arm glittered under the stage lights. She sparkled and glided into position, ready to light each corner, every edge, with her manicured fingertips. After clapping softly, she folded her hands.

Jezalyn clapped too, although her fingers were stubby. Her face absorbed the game show's glow, hungry and distant, which punched a cold hole inside Harlan, a loss he imagined feeling if Jezalyn ever moved or got married or died. Her green eyes opened like a drain, clogged by the flashing colors and wheel's turns. Harlan rooted his boots to the floor, promising himself he would not fall out of the chair in front of his baby sister.

"Buy a vowel! Get an I!" she screamed.

"She should get a U."

"No, she needs the I."

The phone rang. The contestant bought a U, which wasn't in the puzzle.

Jezalyn smirked at Harlan before she answered the phone. "Hey, babydoll. Yep, come through. Love you." She scooted back to the television.

"Wade heading over?" asked Harlan.

"Yeah. Haven't seen much of him lately."

"Why?"

"He's been busy. Tired."

Jezalyn and Wade had been engaged for as long as Mama had been gone, that fucker down on one knee before the cheesecake had even been plated at the wake, but they had yet to decide on flowers, get a dress, or even buy a proper ring. After everyone left the cemetery, Jezalyn came home waggling her finger at Harlan. He'd been drinking all day but remembered he should check for some glitz on her finger. Harlan saw nothing, except for a piece of paper wrapped around her knuckle.

"Where's the ring?"

"It's coming," she sang. "As soon as he sells three more cars, I get to pick it out!" She held her hand out as if she were admiring two carats. "Till then, he gave me this."

Harlan had grabbed her hand to study her finger. A red cigar band. His muscles flushed cold while his fingers clenched.

"Nobody gives my sister trash as a promise for forever." He staggered toward the front door.

"Stop it." She shuffled between him and the door, shoving his shoulders. The hounds jumped up. "Why can't you be happy for me, Harlan?"

"I am happy for you, Jezz." He focused with his good eye. "I'm just looking out for you."

"Yeah? Think you'll find me down the hollow of that bottle?"

He closed his eyes.

"What's at the bottom anyways?"

He'd been sucking from a handle of gin all day, but her words stung like a bumblebee caught in his collar. "If I'm lucky, nothing."

Jezalyn hoisted his gin in the air. "I know why you do it."

Harlan was terrified she'd smash the bottle. It had cost him twenty-four dollars.

"You're afraid that when you get to the end, you'll be all alone. Mama's dead now and the only person who gives one hot shit about you is me." Her face splotched red, her upper lip caught dry on her gums.

"Shut up, Jezz." Harlan steadied himself with a folding chair. "Go on, keep sneaking your booze alone at night in the garage." The hounds barked. "Think you're making Mama proud acting just like her? No one's proud of you." She slammed the handle to the floor with such force that her feet came off the ground.

Harlan had punched right through the wall without feeling anything break. The hounds lunged, but Jezalyn grabbed their collars, dragging them away. He'd seized a stack of takeout napkins and sopped up the gin, scared Jezalyn would forever freeze him in that moment, hating him with her green eyes. But he also saved the wet heap, piling them onto the nearest paper plate knowing full well he'd wring each napkin over his mouth and let the booze drip in as soon as she walked off. They never spoke of it again, letting the incident dart away like a puny fish.

"What time's Wade coming?" asked Harlan.

"After this puzzle," said Jezalyn. She tickled the hounds with ringless fingers.

"I best get working then."

"Sure. I got a big dive tomorrow—trying for forty-five under." She puffed out her cheeks. "Now if you'll excuse me, I'll be with the beautiful people, big brother." She bid him goodnight with a flick of her lighter, swaying with the flame like she was front row to something big.

***

In the garage, Harlan reached behind his workbench for a beer. Cylinders and wires rested on the table, tube socks waiting to be matched. Harlan could refurbish any washing machine in the county, everyone knew that. When a washer gave one last whir and its owner couldn't take another short, the washer found itself out on the curb with a sign that read *Take it, Harlan*. Every month, he'd troll the county, loading old washers into the bed of his pickup. Then he'd spend weeks breathing life into their frayed wires and clunking parts. Antiques dealers would buy the older washers, but Harlan also made house calls and fixed newer models.

A motorcycle burned up to the house. Wade, that big car salesman, didn't even have a car. Was his sister about to hook her wagon to a chump? Thinking about it singed Harlan with an angry thirst, but he never drank gin when finishing a job because he wanted to be sure about his work. A cold one could lube his mind while he fiddled with inlet valves, though. He sipped the beer. He had to be accurate.

Mason's washing machine wasn't draining properly. Harlan checked the drain hose for kinks, tested the lid timer. He tried another beer.

The water pump.

Harlan spent the next two hours labeling hoses and checking for blockages, inspecting the impeller unit for damage. When he hooked it up to his tester hoses, water gushed into the tub, rapids swirling.

Even inside the garage, the night clutched like sweaty fingers around his scruff. He stared into his metallic lake, regretting he'd never learned to swim. When the basket stopped spinning, he dipped his hand into the tub and envisioned the same scribbly blue of his old crayon drawings. Harlan shook off his work boots and clambered onto the lip of the machine, dangling his feet in the cool cartoon water. It lapped against his toes, splashing up his ankles. He climbed in.

***

The morning pecked at Harlan's eyes. Swinging his hangover from the bed, Harlan couldn't remember climbing out of his makeshift hot tub or getting under the covers. He stumbled into the kitchen.

Wade stood shirtless at the toaster with a plate of Pop-Tarts in his hand and a cigarette clutched between his lips. "'Sup."

Harlan felt the smile fall from his face like a loose hem.

"Time to head out and beat the tides." Jezalyn sidled close to Wade, snaking his arm around her shoulders. Her suntan, her giggle, those big green eyes, like she was all lit up by some secret campfire.

"I'm working a halfer today," Wade said to her. "How about I stop by the shore at lunch?"

"Sounds good." Jezalyn bounced up, trying to kiss him on the forehead but was too short and got him on the nostril.

The doorbell rang. Mason stood uneasy on the porch. "About that time, Harlan. Show me what you got."

In the garage, Harlan was grateful to find he'd tidied up his own tools and drained the washing machine. As he demonstrated his repairs to Mason, water shot from two separate hoses, right on cue.

Mason reached into his back pocket and handed Harlan a Ziploc of twenties. "Nice work."

After he left, Harlan sat on his bed smoothing out the twenties. Two hundred dollars. He added eighty to the stack he kept wrapped in his red high school graduation gown, bringing the total to $891.

For the past year, Harlan had been stashing money from his repairs to surprise Jezalyn with a plane ticket all the way to Australia, where the last real pearl divers practiced. Somewhere "off the northwestern coast of Broome." Jezalyn had a wrinkled map of it taped above her headboard. She'd spent hours in her room pinning *National Geographic* photos of copper diving helmets and oyster beds to her chipped yellow walls. Her boss had a friend who'd visited Broome and photographed the divers from the shore. Jezalyn told Harlan about it over pork chops one night.

"They head out in the dinghy at six in the morning and start diving at seven-thirty. Catch the low tide." She was so excited that she couldn't eat. "Then they're underwater in three-hour shifts, scraping around down there." She set her fork on her plate. "Harlan, I want to be one of them."

Harlan stopped chewing. "You already are, sis. Every day, here."

"Don't you want something bigger than here?"

Harlan had never thought about it. His whole life had presented itself to him draped in corduroy and flannel and he accepted it without ever questioning why he still slept in his childhood bed or why his closest friends sat on the same barstools every night. He forgot a lot of other things too, like the name of that girl from last Friday night, but he'd never forgotten what Jezalyn had said. That's when he'd started saving. He couldn't pay much to bury his mama, but he could at least try to help the one person who had ever helped him.

He shoved the money behind some shoeboxes. His closet smelled like it always had, old and small.

***

Harlan entered the liquor store, the rusted silver doorbell jangling behind him. All around him, bottles gleamed, vodka beckoning like fresh well water. Harlan ached.

"The usual, Harlan?" Travis asked.

"Yes, sir." Harlan handed over ten dollars for a fifth of their cheapest gin, hands shaking.

"Threw in some pretzels for such a valued customer."

"I thank you, Travis."

Harlan meandered back to the house along the river, stopping to drink and quack at a trio of ducks. Then he spotted Jezalyn, a bobbing dot on the river's liquid horizon. She gasped at the surface, dodging branches and beer cans. An old Yamaha roared toward the shore, the dust dovetailing. Harlan snuck closer, straining his good eye.

Jezalyn hurried out of the water through the mud, beads of water draping her in river diamonds. Her bag sagged empty.

"Girl," Wade said, gripping his handlebars. "We got to talk."

"Have a surprise for me?" She wiggled her ring finger.

Wade crossed his arms. "I'm kinda struggling. Don't think I can do this anymore."

Harlan slapped at a mosquito near his neck.

"Sorry, Jezz," Wade said. "But I been thinking about it for the last seven months."

"Seven months? You got someone else?"

"Nah." Wade fiddled with the controls on his motorcycle. "You know me."

"Like hell I do."

He rubbed his forehead.

"So this is how it ends," she said. "On a bike. On your lunch break."

"Doesn't matter when I did it. Just knew I had to."

"And you couldn't even get off your bike, do it proper."

Harlan tingled all over. He screwed the lid on tight.

"Is this about T.R. from last summer?" she asked. "Because I swear on my dead mama's bones it's been over."

"No. You already apologized for that."

"Then what? You don't love me anymore?"

"I didn't say that."

"You're not saying much."

"I don't know, I can't explain it, Jezz."

She backed away, slowly, silently, and then ran toward the house, her hounds sprinting with her. Wade started his engine.

Harlan crammed his gin back into the bag and strode out from the bushes. The rock he threw at Wade's disappearing image landed in the dead dry leaves.

***

When Harlan found Jezalyn, she was curled on the kitchen mat, crying the same silent kind of tears she'd cried at Mama's funeral. His guts dropped.

"It's ok, Jezz." He rubbed her back, squeezing away his own tears.

"That bastard."

"I know, I know," Harlan said. Then he paused. "I'll kill him."

"What?" She stared at him until she realized he wasn't kidding.

"I will."

"Christ, don't be so goddamn stupid, Harlan."

In the garage, Harlan shoved his workbench across the floor and gathered all his hidden beers. He shotgunned five of them, the beer hot-footing its way into his head, his fingers, his rage. Then he pocketed a flask for the half-mile walk to the bar.

At the Buck 'n Bronc, Harlan took his stool. Leland nodded and poured him the usual, three shots of their bottom-shelf gin. Harlan settled into his shots.

He had a ritual of lining them up, starting with the fullest. That way, by the time he got to the last one, he was already drinking less. He used to do it darkest to lightest, back when he would mix his liquor. But sticking to gin got the job done fast. Harlan took the first two shots.

"Go on, what's so magical about that big-ass stick?"

"Don't act like you're not dying to find out."

Harlan turned. At the pool table in the corner, Wade stood with an arm slung around a laughing blonde. She was a column of tossed hair, all brazen giggles and arched back.

Harlan slammed his last shot in one go. Then he bore toward the pool table. Squinting with his good eye, he shoved Wade from behind. Before Wade could respond, Harlan socked him in the back of his head. The blonde shrieked. Harlan punched again, missed, squinted, and hooked Wade's chin on the backspin.

"Nobody." Harlan punched until his knuckles were slick, splitting. He was carbon. Feral. "Ain't nobody."

A black boot nailed him in the stomach. Harlan gagged, lurching off Wade. Then a fist barreled into his good eye. He felt the pull of being dragged backward, a caustic white explosion, something wet hitting his cheek.

"You shithead," a woman screeched. Spit landed on him again. "Coming at a grown man with a sucker punch? I pity your mama for making trash like you."

Wade groaned nearby.

"Don't be dumb now," someone with a stern voice said into Harlan's ear. He wasn't sure how long he'd been out or who was there, but his arms were getting pinned behind him. "You know the drill, Harlan. You got the right to remain silent." Two plastic zip ties rigged his wrists and then someone stood him upright. Harlan's good eye strained as he pushed forward into the dusk.

***

In the dream, Harlan was just a tadpole skimming the surface. Jezalyn, wise and smiling, swam through the river next to him. Harlan shot ahead, racing, grinning. Then he was scooped into a bag filled with water, the hard dry world just beyond the skin of the bag. He darted in nervous circles.

Soon it was dark, cool. His world poured down, a smooth plunge, that left him gasping.

"Don't worry, tadpole," Jezalyn called. "I'm right here." She pushed a button.

A waterfall rumbled. Cold water filled the darkness. Harlan relaxed and swam, around and around.

Then, the shake. Harlan couldn't see it, couldn't stop it. But just by the feel of it, he knew he'd be alone, circling the darkness forever.

***

He awoke with an aching bladder and what felt like at least one broken rib. Harlan swallowed. A vein throbbed somewhere behind his good eye, so he jammed his fingers against it to make it stop.

"Warden Ron." Harlan's stomach churned with the effort of yelling. "I have to take a leak."

Ron leaned out of his office. "Turn around and do it then."

Harlan hadn't even thought to turn around. His neck felt taut, rubber bands stretched to snap onto sunburned skin. He closed his eyes, twisting slowly until a dull silver toilet rim came into view. Pushing himself upright, he swallowed the memories that taunted from the back of his throat. The cell, the bars, the slick floor all bent and expanded with each step. He collapsed on the toilet, head spinning in his hands. He held tight so it wouldn't whirl away.

"You done?" asked Ron.

Harlan wanted to sleep right there, as airless as a deflated punchball. The rim felt good behind his thighs, the smell of piss reassuring, and he considered sliding down to the floor so he could rest his forehead against the cool metal. But, instead, he pulled up his pants and stumbled toward the voice. "Yes, boss."

"Post bail or get comfy."

"How much?"

"This time? Public intoxication, disorderly behavior: nine hundred." Ron unlocked the holding cell and walked Harlan to a phone.

The room was hot, save for a desk fan that blew as hard as a kitten's yawn. Sweat dampened his waistband. Harlan didn't want to talk, didn't want his sour breath adding to the warmth in the room. His fingers cramped as he dialed.

"What do you say for yourself?" Jezalyn said, the letter-lighting sounds of *Wheel of Fortune* echoing in the background.

"Is it night already, Jezalyn?"

"Yeah, and you're interrupting."

"I'm in jail." His words spun away like a kite in a tornado.

"Wade told me."

Harlan closed his eyes. "I'm no fool, Jezalyn."

"Sure sounds like you might be. That was his cousin Sharice."

"You don't believe that. Have you met her?"

"What do you fucking want?"

"In the back of my closet's a stack of money. It's wrapped up in my red graduation gown. Can you get it?"

She set the phone down. Harlan could hear the chimes from the game show, light and hopeful. He flinched at the thought of Vanna's shimmer.

"This is a shitload of money, Harlan."

"Can I borrow ten bucks?"

"That's all I've got right now."
"Thanks, Jezz. I owe you."
"Yeah, you do."

***

Jezalyn met him in the parking lot, and they walked to her old silver Sebring. "Don't know how you got all that money. Don't want to know. But I'm proud you didn't drink it."

Inside, the upholstery smelled of stale Parliaments.

Wade sneered at him from the front seat, his face bruised, lower lip puffy and purpled. "Hey, loser. How was jail?"

"Worth it," Harlan said.

"Sucker punches are for pussies."

"You'd know."

"Stop it." Jezalyn lit a cigarette and handed it to Wade. She lit another for herself. "Wade told me everything."

"Right, 'his cousin,'" Harlan said.

"We grew up together," Wade said. "Mind your business."

Harlan concentrated on not getting sick out the window. "Jezz, come on."

"Shut up, Harlan. I don't need advice from a drunk-ass. And let me tell you, you better not act up at the wedding."

"Whose wedding?"

"Ours, next month," Wade said, his face snagged between a wince and a smirk.

"I don't believe it."

"Don't matter what you think anymore, brother. You're out of the house after this."

"What? Where am I supposed to go?"

"Not our problem," Jezalyn said. "You had almost nine hundred bucks hidden away. I'm sure you can come up with it again."

Stagnate with heat and smoke, the air overpowered him like Uncle Joel's big-bosomed lady friends writhing with the Sunday spirit. Then, like now, he needed air. An escape. Jezalyn passed their street.

"You missed it," Harlan said.

"No, I didn't."

She pulled the car through the dogwoods to their old childhood swimming hole. The sunset smeared across the horizon, a cracked quail egg sliding on the plate of sky. She reached behind her, yanking a plastic bag from under Harlan's boot. "Get up."

Harlan groaned. "You know I can't."

"Then you get to sit there and watch." She dropped her cigarette butt into an empty Mountain Dew can in the console. Wade got out of the car and waited for her by the hood. As they walked to the shore together, Wade tucked her under his shoulder, blowing a low cloud of smoke above her.

Jezalyn maneuvered through the flickering waves of heat toward the river's edge, the empty bag trailing behind her like the train on a gown. Harlan watched until she was just a muted sparkle against the curve of the searing sun, a flare streaming out of the horizon, a bag billowing, a woman submerged.

CASUALTIES OF THE VAINGLORIOUS

THURSDAY

Walter ran a hand over the shellacked perfection of his hair. Yes. The Vaseline gleamed on his front teeth, keeping his lips off his gums. With everything in order up top, he smoothed his fingers down his shirt and made sure the horse was in the barn below.

"Thirty seconds," Albert warned.

"Am I okay?" Walter asked.

Jackie rushed over. "Not yet."

Walter panicked while she powdered the sheen from his forehead. Angles to avoid looking chunky. Chin out and down. And where were his note cards?

"Twenty seconds," said Albert.

Walter dodged Jackie's brush. "Not too much." He didn't need setting powder clinging to his jowls. This wasn't an audition for *The Golden Girls*! (Though he was definitely a Dorothy.)

"Ten seconds."

Walter grabbed the fluorescent green Zipper 2020 vacuum. It was heavier than he expected and he worried lifting it would make him even sweatier. "Why didn't anyone tell me how heavy this would be?"

Then Albert pointed at him, so Walter exhaled into his trusted powerwatt smile. His note cards might be missing, but he could go off the cuff like a regular Johnny Carson.

"Welcome back to the Home Shopping Network, folks. Ever wished you could suck away all the garbage in your life?"

***

"That was so cool, Dad. Twelve hundred vacuums! I watched the whole thing."

"Thanks, champ." In his dressing room, Walter scrutinized his profile while he chatted on the phone with his son, Ash. "Just another day at the office."

"Sure, with five million people tuned in," Ash said.

Actually, it was only half a million. "How was school?"

"Okay. The grilled cheese was pretty good today. And yeah, I finished all my homework."

Walter smiled. Ash monitored his segments after middle school each day, charting how much his father had sold and if he'd broken any personal bests. Walter loved Ash's phone calls, especially after a good day's sell. It made him feel like he was doing something right.

"I better go, Mom's home now," Ash said. "Can we do some Monopoly tonight? I need to practice before Saturday."

Walter flinched. Ash had qualified for the Western Youth Monopoly Championships up in Charlotte and wanted both parents with him, which meant they'd all be flying from Tampa together. This also meant Walter would be taking a vacation with his ex-wife, something they hadn't done since their honeymoon in the Outer Banks twelve years ago. And since Walter and Simone had been too broke to travel during most of their marriage, it would be their first family trip together, a fact that both exhilarated and debilitated him. He'd been doing extra sit-ups every morning for the past month, loading up on spinach at dinner. He was also fully prepared (*Princess Bride* quote, a swooning kiss) if Simone happened to suggest getting back together.

"Can't wait. See you soon, little man."

"I'm already five-six, Dad," Ash said. "I'll be bigger than you soon enough."

***

Walter wrote down the official grand total on a note card so he wouldn't forget it: *twelve hundred and thirty-two vacuums!!!!* He added a happy face and three stars. It was a stunning new personal record. And just in time to ask for his contract to be renewed on Monday.

"Devotion should be rewarded," Walter would say to kick off his yearly review. Pop had used that very line on Ma whenever he wanted to host the next poker night and it never failed.

Walter tucked the card into his wallet. Between alimony and legal fees and having to rent a condo, money had been tight after the divorce. If he could lock down another three-year contract, he could start saving for his retirement. Plus he could take Ash on a road trip to Mount Rushmore—the wall of giants! And after offloading over twelve hundred vacuums, wasn't he a giant in his own right, too? His photo would sit atop the breakroom's Supersellers Hall of Fame soon enough! And now, it was time for the man who hosted, nay, dominated, the primo shift to assert himself.

Scoring the coveted daytime slot three years ago made Walter feel like he'd won an arm-wrestling match. At the time, Simone had just put the kibosh on their marriage. Right when he'd been on the toughest shift, too: pushing juicers on insomniacs and hoarders from midnight until four in the morning. But after his record topaz sales during Gem-a-palooza, the network thought he could be a real hit with stay-at-home moms. Sure enough, he'd knocked the ratings out of the park during the Summer Purse Blowout and then again during Cointasia.

"You've got that Old Hollywood appeal, Walter," his boss Ethan had said. "It makes the ladies want to spend, spend, spend."

Like he was Cary Grant! And Ethan would know: he was twenty-two years younger than Walter and wore a newsboy cap to work every day. INDOORS. The balls.

Walter took the compliment to heart, minus the "old" part of course, and repeated it to himself whenever he woke up feeling lonely. Which was pretty often. A gangly mess in junior high, two hundred fifty pounds straining against his prom cummerbund, divorced now, Walter felt like a set of golf clubs that just wouldn't sell. But deep down, he knew that's why he was a good salesman: he wasn't any different from the bored broads who called in. Everyone just wanted to be seen.

Which got him pondering the future. Here he was, fifty-seven, slim, and moving vacuums on cable television at record rates. He could still jog without taping his knees, his nose hairs were now under control, and he'd been practicing a dance move he could do while holding a plate of shrimp at the holiday party.

Hoo boy, he was witty, classy, roosting at the top where he belonged! And if the numbers showed women loved him, who was he to argue with math?

With some time before the all-staff meeting, Walter practiced emoting in his mirror. Here I am, so joyful that you're ordering cheese knives for your mother, just in time for the holidays. Now I'm surprised, but happy, to learn you're calling in for a second time today, you mischievous minx. He'd made it a daily habit to test different postures and ensure he was working his best side. He also did twenty chin thrusts to keep a tight neck.

Then he saw it. Walter leaned closer and pawed his hair. White, white, Arctic white, the very breath of the reaper icing his follicles. My god, he was only fifty-seven!

Jackie knocked. "Good hustle today, Walt," she said, setting up her manicure station.

"Thanks," he said. As soon as Jackie glanced down, he returned to fixating on his grays. When had his father become a silver fox? A meticulous man, Pop had used travel scissors to perfect his mustache every Saturday morning.

"It takes two things to be a real man," Pop would say. "A good shave and a beautiful woman."

So every morning before preschool, Walter climbed a stack of phone books and stood at the sink next to Pop. Careful and precise, he dragged a red toy razor across his own cheeks, mimicking his father. Then they'd slap their faces with aftershave. Walter still punctuated his mornings with Old Spice, a tradition he couldn't wait to teach Ash.

He soaked his fingertips in the warm soapy water. Was that a liver spot on his hand?

"Everything all right?" Jackie asked.

"What's the best way to deal with this?" He pointed to his hair.

"Hide it. Everyone does."

Walter frowned. "Hats look silly on me."

She stared at him. "No, you can fix it with some color."

"Absolutely not. I refuse to hit the beds!" Walter had stopped tanning last year because he didn't want to get skin cancer and pass away before Ash got his driver's permit.

"Relax. You just need to dye. They'll fix you up at the salon."

"I'm not made of money! What do people like you do?"

She sighed. "Go to the drugstore." While she buffed his nails, she listed the different brands he could buy.

"Excellent." Walter studied his reflection in the shiny half-moons of his fingernails. Was it waxing? Waning? Either way, how strange to see himself so small.

Albert ducked in the dressing room. "Ready for the meeting, guys?"

And then an idea began to burn. They only had all-hands meetings when something big was about to happen. Could it be his promotion? Were they beating him to the punch? It was the perfect day for it. Walter reminded himself he must appear humbled, yet surprised. Plus, there might be jelly doughnuts.

"Absotootley!" he said, pumping his fist in solidarity. He followed Albert.

The conference room was stuffed with everyone from the camera team to catering. He waved to the ones he knew, nodded at the others, but apparently it was packed with party poopers who couldn't be bothered to acknowledge him. Jeesh. Ethan sat at the head of the table, fidgeting. He wasn't wearing his cap or even a smile. Walter's stomach lurched. That better not mean he'd have to start pushing Tupperware. Plastic housewares would end him. How could anyone possibly make them sound special? Well, if anyone could, it'd be Walter. That was the challenge of being on live television: it forced you to think right there on the spot, like you could get pantsed at any second.

"Folks, we've got unsettling news," Ethan said.

"Is the coffee machine broken again?" Walter quipped. He waited for giggles, but the room felt strangely airless.

Ethan cleared his throat. "I'm sorry to announce that the network has been bought out."

Jackie gasped. "What does that mean?"

"Sadly, most of us will be Sprout employees come Monday."

Walter's coworkers were agape. Sprout Entertainment was their biggest rival, a network that had secured the reality TV sector, their stronghold on Middle Americans with sob stories, all basset-eyed, vying for singing supremacy. Sprout didn't even sell anything live! And at night? They just looped infomercials for abdominal exercise machines until the sun came up. Their hosts were breasty young blondes.

"In these envelopes are your reassignments," Ethan said as the HR lady placed manila envelopes in front of each employee. "This is a real shock, even to me."

Jackie began to bawl.

"You'll have to clean out your offices and dressing rooms by the end of the day. Again, I'm so sorry, but you can blame the shitheads at Sprout."

As the lead daytime host, Walter knew he should demonstrate leadership and sympathy. "I'm very sorry this is happening to you all. If there's anything I can do, please don't hesitate to ask." He closed his eyes and lowered his head, the HR lady swishing past.

"Open your eyes, Walter," Jackie said. "We're not alone."

"How very true, Jackie. You are not alone."

"Take a look," Albert muttered. "You're one of us now."

When Walter opened his eyes, he was greeted by an envelope. He popped up in the conference chair. By the time he saw "retained by HSN" with "administrative role" next to a pay rate that was half of what he currently earned, Walter knew his mouth would drive while his brain rode shotgun. "Oh, come now. This is a mistake."

"Unfortunately Sprout doesn't think so," Ethan said.

"I'm certain everyone who's staying would disagree."

Ethan kneaded his temples. "Don't make this worse, Walter."

"What?"

"Sprout's not taking everyone."

"Who else isn't going? Jackie?"

"You," Ethan shouted. "Sprout's taking everyone but you."

Walter stood. "That's silly. How am I supposed to do my segments?"

"There won't be any. You're going to stay at HSN as the new head consultant in Customer Service."

"Consultant?" Walter fumbled for his accomplishments, but his hands were too shaky to grab his wallet. "I sold more than twelve hundred vacuums today. I've been here for years. I sweat through my shirt working so hard." He opened his coat to reveal wet rings blooming under his armpits. "Wait, wait." Preparing for the balloons and knowing grins, Walter stood tall to appear thinner for the camera. "Where are they?"

"Who?"

"The prank crew! Before you give me my promotion?"

"Jesus, there's no promotion."

"But devotion should be rewarded! I deserve a big raise."

"We all do," Jackie cried.

"This isn't about you, Walter."

Walter scanned his coworkers' faces. They'd stopped crying and most of them were shaking their heads.

"You're right." He closed his eyes.

"Okay. As I was saying—" Ethan started.

"It's about my son, who's too young to feed and clothe himself. What should I tell him?" Walter reached for the phone in the middle of the table. "In fact, why don't we call him and let him know right now?" He dialed Ash's cell phone number.

"I didn't have a choice," Ethan said. "The future is with Sprout."

"For Pete's sake, please tell me being demoted to some dumbass admin role at the unmarketable age of fifty-seven is a joke."

"Dad?" a voice called from the speakerphone.

"Ash?" Walter couldn't figure out which button would mute their conversation. "Sorry, kiddo, we've got the wrong number here."

"It's the light blue button," Ethan hissed.

"Why are you talking like that, Dad?"

There were two different blue buttons. Walter pushed the top one. The volume increased. "Everything's fine, champ. I'll call you later tonight, all right?"

"You're scaring me—"

Walter slammed the receiver down. The dial tone echoed loud and flat from the speakerphone.

"Happy now?" Ethan asked.

"No." Walter said. "I quit."

***

An hour later, Walter wandered the drug store aisles, fuming. He was an industry giant! He would handle his unemployment, just like he'd handled his divorce. Well, hopefully better than that. And with fewer tubs of Ben & Jerry's. He quickly reimagined himself as a dapper cruise ship passenger, tan and adoring on a romantic stroll in the French Riviera. Feeling more confident already, he grabbed a bottle of Old Spice for Ash.

Walter considered boxes of hair dye. *Why let your gray get in the way?* one brand asked. He didn't have an answer. But the lumberjack on front, with his winter tan and big-game hunter grin, might know. And for six measly bucks! Walter studied the instructions. His hair was the color of potting soil, which made him a True Brown on the box's color scale. But was he more Chestnut? Coffee? Copper? He'd never thought of his hair color in relation to nuts or metals. How does anyone know these things? Should he know these things?

"Could you excuse me, miss?" he asked a nearby clerk.

The girl, enrobed in enough kohl to make Cleopatra jealous, exhaled a sigh of such magnitude that Walter instantly recalled season twenty-nine of *Days of Our Lives*. Scowling, she worked a blue knot of gum, appearing to count the seconds until she could huff paint fumes with her friends in the parking lot.

"Whoa," Walter said, getting a close-up of her. He hadn't meant to say it aloud, but her features jutted like a sidewalk crack he'd just tripped over. "Wrong color," he said, shaking the box as he backed away. "My mistake."

A woman shrieked behind him. "Walter! Owen! Wilkinson!"

Walter automatically flashed his powerwatt grin and blindly turned around. "Yes?"

The store pharmacist strode toward him like a bull to the cape. "I bought a Tiffany-style desk lamp from you last month."

"Wonderful," he said. "And how do you like it?"

"You were so right. The multicolored shade really warms up my reading corner. My spaniels and I can't thank you enough."

Walter didn't remember saying that, but it certainly sounded clever. He tried to appear bashful.

"I'm glad," he said, glancing at her nametag. "While I've got your attention, Marla, could you do me a favor?" He enjoyed meeting strangers—making someone laugh felt like a high five from himself to himself for being so suave. Walter also kept fifteen signed headshots in his glove box, just in case. "Which shade is best for my ugly mug?"

"With your looks, you could do anything," Marla said, beaming.

Walter grinned. She was attractive, maybe in her mid-forties, and although she could stand to drop thirty pounds, she had a pretty good face.

"I don't mean to be forward," she said, "but I adore you. I never miss your segments and my garage is filled with things you personally recommended. My husband hates you for it."

"It's my good fortune that people like you care."

"You're really something, Walter. You could roll a turd in powdered sugar and sell it as a donut. I'd eat it."

He flinched. "Oh?"

"I'd choose Chestnut for you. A yummy, thick brown." Marla closed her eyes, drifting off into an intimate moment.

He panicked. "Chestnut it is. Thank you very much." If she was flirting, it was exactly why dating scared him. He hadn't done it in years, and he was awed by people who dated regularly, like on Sprout's boozy dating shows, the couples half-naked in hot tubs while the water churned with chlamydia and regret. Their sloppy seductions disgusted him, but also made him jealous. Walter had rarely dated when he was younger, and he couldn't believe his luck when someone as beautiful as Simone had given him her real phone number at the supermarket that day. Now he often fretted, open-eyed in the night, about how he'd die and if he'd be alone when it happened.

"Enjoy your new light," he said.

"You know I will."

Walter swore her tongue did a teeny cobra flicker as he hustled to the cashier. But he had fans! And with fans, even creepy ones, he could be the giant Ash needed.

***

Squirting brown dye along his hairline, Walter was careful not to stain his collar. He was determined to look handsome for their family vacation. Mysterious, even. And definitely five years younger.

Walter had custody of Ash on the weekends, so every Thursday evening at six, Simone dropped Ash at Walter's apartment, where father and son would descend on their holy trinity: Sloppy Joes, *The Simpsons*, and discussions about Ash's Young Entrepreneur's club. Walter cherished his weekly chance to be a dad.

The doorbell chimed while he finished blow-drying his hair. Walter whirled hairspray around his head, flashed a grin in the mirror, and scurried to the front door. Simone and Ash gawked at him.

"Wow!" Ash said.

She raised an eyebrow. "Looks good, Walt."

He considered his ex-wife. Throughout the ten years of their marriage, Simone had adorned herself in what he considered "polygamy chic": loads of dumpy floral dresses topped with oppressive spritzes of rose water. Since the divorce, though, she'd raised her hemlines and traded petunias for cleavage. She stood smiling, zippered into a tight green dress. Simone looked like a stack of hundred-dollar bills. Though she worked as a pastry chef at a hotel downtown, her skin-flick outfits made him wonder what else she was doing. And why did she smell like sandalwood now?

"Where are you off to tonight?" Walter asked.

"Paolo's surprising me for our six-month anniversary."

Walter swallowed back a gag. "He stuck around?"

"Be nice," she said, eyeing him. "We're happy."

"Paolo's cool, Dad."

Walter turned to pull his key out of the lock, hiding his crumbling face. "Well, I'm glad you like my cool new 'do."

And with that, he officially ambered himself as prehistoric. He was pretty sure he'd made finger guns when he said it, too. Oh, how he prayed he'd spontaneously combust. Walter had cringed at several memories throughout his life, but the sour cherry on top had been when Simone demanded a divorce. They'd been bickering for months, fighting the same three fights that couples have when they refuse to admit they were strangers at the altar: how to spend money, how to talk to each other from different planets, and how much sexy time they should schedule each month (or season, if someone mysteriously had yet another headache/allergic reaction/sunburn/gassy episode).

"I may regret marrying you," Simone had growled when she stormed Chipotle to serve him with papers on his lunch break, "but I don't regret our son. I won't let you ruin that relationship, too."

"I'm not trying to ruin anything," he'd said. "I still love you."

"Let's keep it clean: joint custody, no drama." Divorce had sent her constant indecision on a detour.

"Of course," he said. "Just promise you won't take him away from me. Please."

She dabbed her eyes. "I promise. He admires you so much."

Walter pictured his son, skinny arms outstretched for a hug, his silly trapezoid of a smile. Ash's laugh was the best sound in the world. Walter teared at the thought of losing him. "Will you sit with me and hash this out?"

Simone shook her head. "I know you're a good man. But we can't force something that's not right."

"Soulmates fight. It happens."

"You're not seeing things clearly, Walter." She slipped the paperwork next to his grilled chicken salad and then walked out.

Walter had felt like he'd been sucker punched in a dream only to wake up with a real shiner. Once Simone served him, they vowed they would never fight in front of Ash. Then, weeks later, after Ash stared at his dino nuggets while his parents screamed about splitting the Charlie Chaplin DVDs, one of Simone's employees delivered an elegant two-tiered cake to the set. Walter strode over, smug she'd decided to apologize. Simone had anchored handmade roses along the edges just like their wedding cake, but instead of white, they were asphalt black. At the top was a bride figurine, standing alone, arms raised in victory. Below that, a crimson trail led down to the groom, plunged headfirst into a sugary pool of red. She'd also taken the time to etch *Suck It* in her elegant calligraphy.

This public display of anger had been humiliating. In front of all his friends and potential lovers! How long had it taken her to make? Was there poison filling inside? When he lunged to throw it away, his thumb accidentally scraped the edge. She was such a talented baker. He licked his fingertip. As soon as the buttercream touched his tongue, he decided that if he were going to be poisoned, he'd at least like to die with something sweet on his lips. So he ate the entire top tier in the privacy of his dressing room. When he woke up the next morning and realized he hadn't died, he decided to relinquish his anger.

Walter gestured to his living room. "Care to stay?" He'd filled a new vase with iridescent glass pebbles and a tall silk orchid, proof he could decorate just fine without her.

"I can't. But I brought treats." She handed him a box of homemade carrot ginger muffins, fresh from the oven.

MOUTH

The goodies were healthy, so obviously she'd noticed he'd trimmed down. Which means she must've been checking him out. But did she think he didn't have enough money to buy breakfast?

"Thanks. Hey, big news," his mouth said. "I've got an interview with Sprout tomorrow."

"Sprout? Your mortal enemy?"

"Indeed. I figured why not give HSN a run for their money?" The lie parachuted from his mouth.

"Good for you, Walt."

"It's a gamble, but I could collect quite a bit more."

"That's wonderful. It's great to see you so excited."

Time to shoot his shot, courtesy of a little nostalgia. "Are you ready for North Carolina? It's been quite a while since we've been there."

"Can we go to the Outer Banks?" Ash asked.

"I wish, champ." Walter studied Simone.

"It's too far," she said, kissing Ash. "Make sure you practice a bunch until Saturday." As she gave Walter a side hug, his nose skimmed her curls. She smelled like warm honey, so he envisioned a brigade of vindictive skunks to redirect his blood flow while she drove away.

"What was that phone call about today, Dad?" Ash asked.

"It was weird."

"I'm sorry you had to hear that work talk. They're making some changes, but this guy's going to be a-okay."

"But aren't you the most important one there?"

Walter had never loved his son more. "Don't worry, I've got a trick up my sleeve." He smiled.

"I can't believe you're going to work at Sprout! They have the best shows."

Walter winced. "Let's not say anything to Mom, though."

"Why?"

"I don't want to worry her. I'll wait until it's all settled." Walter tried to keep his voice light so Ash wouldn't think he hated Simone. He didn't. It was just that he couldn't believe he was a divorcé now. After twelve happy—at least tolerable—years of marriage.

Inside the apartment, Ash slid his backpack onto a TV tray.

"How's the Monopoly going?" Walter asked.

"Good. I got a flyer for you." Ash pulled out a wrinkled yellow paper, blasted with the words *Western Division Youth Monopoly Championship Finals! Brought to you on Channel 2!* "I can't believe I might be on TV! You'll have to give me some tips."

"I'd love that."

"And Mom bought me a new shirt to wear."

Walter cued his powerwatt smile. "Fantastic." He rifled through the drugstore bag. "I got something for you, too."

"What's this for?" Ash asked, studying the aftershave.

Walter pointed to the jagged black trail fuzzing above Ash's mouth. "It's time for you to start shaving. I can show you."

"Mom already bought me an electric shaver."

"Do you know how to use it?"

"Yeah. Paolo helped me."

"Oh. Well, I could teach you how to use a razor."

"I like Paolo's shaver."

"Cool!" Walter swallowed his devastation. "It'll be here if you want it." He pointed to the Monopoly board. "Now why don't you show me what you're really made of."

Ash's face, stinging with whiteheads, lit with a hope that Walter could not deny. Ash was wading out into the teenage years, drifting further from their limited time together when Walter just wanted him close to shore. He'd never forget Ash's very first word (appropriately "doo-doo" during a late-night diaper change, Walter so deliriously tired he thought he was imagining it and then too deliriously happy to sleep after it). And Ash's first tottering steps, the drooling delight on his face as he collapsed into Walter's hug. Now his son was shuffling the Title Deeds and hotel figurines that Walter had grown up with. Pop loved Monopoly, and since he died when Ash was a toddler, Walter thought it'd be a nice surprise to tuck Pop's heirloom board under the Christmas tree last year. Ash had been hooked ever since.

As Ash stacked the deeds, Walter studied the board. A question mark. A light bulb. A sparkling diamond.

"What do you want to be, Dad?"

"What are the options again?"

Ash held up a miniature man posed atop a four-legged animal. "How about the horse guy?"

"You're positive that's not a donkey?"

"Positive. I'll be the Scottie."

Walter rolled the dice and moved the horse rider over four spaces, landing on the Income Tax square.

"Okay, state your total worth, Dad."

Walter glanced ahead to the other squares, his eyes resting on the angry glare of a figure behind bars. Underneath were the words *Just Visiting*.

***

FRIDAY

After dropping off Ash at school, Walter pulled into the Sprout parking lot, hopped up on three mugs of Yuban and Aretha Franklin's greatest hits. He felt sharp in his navy suit and butter-yellow tie, a dense coating of Vaseline smeared across his teeth. Ready to take on the performance of his life! His list of accomplishments was folded safe inside his wallet, and although he'd nicked his neck shaving, he'd sopped it up with bits of paper towel. He was brimming with Old Spice and gentlemanly appeal.

As he walked, he reminded himself that getting demoted was just the push he needed. It couldn't have been easy to retire their top seller, and in a sense, they were admitting, *You deserve bigger, Walter. Go, reach higher*. How sad. Yet, how brave.

"Can I help you, sir?" the receptionist asked.

"Yes, it's about the Sprout merger. I am, or I was, the top-selling daytime host at the Home Shopping Network? I'm sure you know." He winked. "I'm interested in discussing my options with Sprout."

"Do you have an appointment?"

"I don't. But I'm hoping that's where you can help." He slid a ten-dollar bill across the counter. It was his lunch budget for the week, but worth the sacrifice.

"I don't give out change, sir."

"No, no, it's for you." He turned up his powerwatt grin. "Have a seat, please."

"Are you sure?" He added some ones and pushed it all toward her.

"I'm certain."

"Thank you." He quietly crumpled the money inside his suit pocket and sat very still.

She spoke into her headset. Then she turned away, speaking softer. "How long? Damn." She removed her headset as she addressed Walter. "It'll be a while."

"I've got all day. But I'll let you know if I have to go to the bathroom." He regretted it as soon as he heard his lips say it. Grabbing a *Forbes*, Walter grimaced at the same millionaire's profile until he was buzzed through the doors an hour later.

The conference room had exposed beams and sleek white furniture. Jiminy Christmas, why hadn't he gone for hip jeans and a sport coat? The mere thought of all that pinspotting highlighting his frumpiness was making his pits damp again and he was just about to lift his arm and waft when a muscular man with a smooth neck entered the room.

"Jared Douglas, veep," he said, waving a foil-wrapped burrito. "What can we do you for?"

Walter inhaled as they sat down. He'd memorized the reasons he should be hired in order of importance: 1) he had an expansive female fan base that would follow him with their customer loyalty and money; 2) he had seven years of on-set experience; and 3) he could hawk over twelve hundred vacuums in one shift. As a backup: 4) he did not believe in Botox but would get it if professionally required.

"Hungry?" Jared asked.

"No, thank you."

"You've got something on your neck there."

Walter's hand rushed to the cut and peeled a bloodied scrap from his skin.

"Try electric," Jared said.

"Yes, I've heard."

"Anyways, hit me."

Walter tented his trembling hands. "I don't have a ton of experience doing reality, but—"

Jared shoved the burrito in his mouth and somehow didn't lose a single bean.

"I need a job."

"Brother, I hear you. And I'm so sorry for your loss," Jared said, wiping his mouth. "I'm sure it wasn't easy to pop by. But TV's all about the reality sector now. Viewers want youth and excitement, the ability to judge and feel superior from the comfort of their own sweatpants." He took Walter gently by the shoulder. "I appreciate you thinking of us. But people can buy their purses off the internet. Come by when you feel more comfortable doing reality." Opening the door, Jared steered Walter down the plush, soundless hallway, stopping outside the kitchen. "Hey, grab yourself a bro-ito! Best of luck!"

Walter hurried past the receptionist, careful not to crush the carne asada quietly warming his pocket.

***

SATURDAY

The next morning, taxis dodged pedestrians and roller bags outside the terminal at Tampa International. Walter huddled in a corner behind a trash can while Ash stood at the curb, neck craned, scouring the crowd for Simone.

"Please, Ethan," Walter whispered into his phone. "It was a mistake. I know that now."

"Do you see her, Dad?"

Walter motioned that he needed a minute. "I'll do anything." He felt his eyes burn, so he put his sunglasses on. Then he turned deeper into the corner. "I'm begging you." He wiped his eyes. "Ok, great. Thank you, Ethan. I really appreciate this. Until then." He hung up and turned back toward Ash. But he was gone.

"Ash?"

Spinning around, Walter felt sick. "Ash! Champ!" Ash was gone. It was happening. He rushed through the crowd, loss pounding in his ears.

"Have you seen a boy, twelve?" Walter asked an older couple. "Brown hair, acne?"

"Sorry," they said. "Wait, aren't you on TV?"

Walter ran past them, knees aching. "Ash! Where are you? Ash!"

He'd lost the most important person in his life. His son was gone and it was his fault and his ex-wife would know he was still a failure. All his fears were coming true. He had nothing and was alone.

"Ash? Don't move, wherever you are!"

"Dad, relax. I'm right here."

Walter spun to find Simone and Ash staring at him. "What a relief."

"Did you think we left?"

"I was terrified."

"We were here the whole time. Didn't you see us?"

"I'm sorry." He cleared his throat. "I was all wrapped up. But I'm here now."

"Cool. Let's go!" Ash said.

Heart pounding in his ears, Walter followed his son and ex-wife across the terminal carpet. There they were: his family. Their first family vacation.

Simone sniffed Ash. "Are you wearing aftershave?"

Ash shrugged. "I just tried it on."

Walter smiled.

There was no one waiting in the security line as the three of them slipped off their sneakers. Walter led the shoeless charge, followed by Simone and then Ash. He yanked out bins for each of them.

"Just put them all in the same one," Simone said. "It'll be easier." She nestled all three pairs of shoes together in the bin.

His heart ached. "Good idea."

"How'd your meeting go?" she asked.

"Hate to brag, but I knocked it out of the park."

"That's fantastic," she said.

"Did you rip them a new one, Dad?"

"Language, Ash," Walter said. "I simply went in there and showed them who's boss." He chuckled for effect. "I'll never forget their faces!"

"Good, because it sounded like you were getting fired or something," Ash said.

Flashing his powerwatt grin, Walter avoided Simone's eyes. "No, no."

"What's he talking about?" Simone asked.

"They're doing a reorg at work. So I decided against Sprout. Think I'll stick with what I know."

Simone's eyes softened. "I'm sorry, Walter."

As he hurried through the metal detector, a buzzer sounded with flashing red lights. The TSA agent stared him down.

"Sir, your wallet. It's in your back pocket."

"My mistake." Walter tossed it toward the bucket, but missed, and all his credit cards spilled out, along with a toothpick, two pennies, the note card with his vacuum grand total on it, and the cropped photo of him and Simone laughing in the limo after their wedding. Walter scrambled to grab everything and when he stood, he struck the crown of his head on the table.

"Are you all right?" Simone asked.

"I'm great!"

Inside the air chamber, he raised his arms like a stick-up. The slow whir of air was too weak to provide any relief to his pits and he prayed Simone was too busy inspecting a hangnail to notice him drenched in sweat. When the agent waved him through, Walter stepped out and discreetly mopped his face, waiting for his items to arrive on the conveyer belt.

At the entry to the chamber, while Simone fumbled with her cell phone and laptop back at the bins, Ash hesitated. "Can I go?"

From a distance, Ash appeared surprisingly older. Taller, more muscular. His son. The soft puff of toddler fingers reaching up for him at the crosswalk. The time he choked on an ice cube at Burger King. His first Pinewood Derby. The moment he didn't need a steadying hand on the bike seat anymore.

Walter sat down alone on the bench, gazing up at his boy. "It's okay, Ash," he said. "Go on ahead."

THE OVATION

Hops McGee flipped through the floodlit sky and prayed the padded barrel would be within crawling distance when he landed. He hung, suspended in the slow whirl between the crowd's gasp and the bull's snort, his shoulders tucked, preparing for the white explosion behind his eyes. Then, the thud.

Ribs heaving in his rodeo jersey, Hops smacked his left thigh. Dust puffed from his shorts, the greasy stink of saddle oil and manure thick in the barrel. But he could still bend his knees, open his jaw.

He waited inside while the crowd's muffled cheers enveloped him. His time spent curled in the barrel, alone after a big save, was his favorite part of bullfighting, and Hops sopped up each moment longer than he should. He imagined it was like hearing guests whispering at a surprise party he already knew about. Or like being a real cowboy.

Cooter and Duke, the two younger clowns, pounded on his barrel, leaning in with white grins hooped around their unsmiling lips. "Whenever you're ready, Princess."

"Just need a second."

Hops shut his eyes, relishing the echo. At thirty-six, he wouldn't be able to do it much longer. There were too many torn ligaments now, a shoulder that couldn't be trusted. But clowning in Montana, his home state, where people were learning his name, sure felt like winning. He poked his head out of the barrel, got a few more applause. Jitterbugging back to his side of the arena, he added in some box steps while the audience clapped to the beat. People loved his goofball dances, the more loose-limbed, the better. It was what he was known for, more than his bullfighting, he feared. Hops tossed in a belly roll for laughs. After taking a bow, he grabbed his battered Stetson from the ground and bent it back into shape. A hoof print had soiled the brim.

"Quite a scare out there, Hops!" the announcer, Russ, chuckled.

Hops flashed a thumbs-up. "I'm no scaredy cat."

Doubling down: another thing he'd gotten good at.

***

Between bulls, his best friend practiced behind the chutes. Cody Curtis, trim and strong in his finest chaps, jerked in a phantom ride, his body roiling with each imagined hind kick. Even with two slipped discs and a lacerated calf muscle, Cody kept his cool. He stood tall and toothy for every photo. Superfans, hot chicks, rugrats all wanted photos with Cody. Snickering teenage boys were the only ones who lined up for Hops.

Cody warmed up out back so he wouldn't be distracted by his long line of fans. A win tonight would secure his spot in the finals and a shot at ten thousand bucks. Just by the way Cody moved, Hops knew what he must be thinking: that's enough cash. Cody kept his left hand in the air. Ten thousand could move the whole family—Callie, little Colton, and Cody—out of Montana down to Amarillo where he could get to living the life.

MOUTH

"This shit's amateur hour," Cody had been saying for the past year. "These guys, all beat down. Me and you could hit it big in Texas, so yank that thumb out your ass and come with."

Hops had spent thousands on his own medical bills just to make sure Cody stayed safe on the dirt. Was happy to do it. But the thought of a younger, faster clown taking his place made him want to break things. He had to stay where he was good. Cody made him good.

"Amarillo's packed twenty-deep with clowns," Hops said.

"And?"

His best friend tightened the knuckle-grip of his right hand. Cody was twenty-six and in his prime. Cody could only go up.

"I'm just a big fish in this pond, Cody. You're the shark."

***

"Weeeeeeeee ready for the next one, folks?" Hops yelled into the microphone bud attached to his ear. It was new, something the pros on TV used. Hops had been bullfighting for seven years. Never any good at breaking horses, but the best at being awkward, so he put it to good use with goofy dances to make the local crowds laugh. Now he was practically a professional.

"Backlash is a-raring to go!" bellowed Russ.

A gray bull spasmed inside the bucking chute. One guy tugged the frayed ends of its tail, another slapped its snout. A third guy strained, wrapping rope around his own mangled cattleman fingers. The bull had weighed in at sixteen hundred pounds.

Hops also recognized Cody's helmet in the chute. Bright orange, so my kid knows when to start cheering, he'd said when he bought it.

"Gotta go, gotta go, gotta rodeo, Russ!" Hops yelled. "Let's welcome Backlash with some cowboy hospitality." *Cowboy.* It fired him up to say it, just to have the word in his mouth.

Everyone booed.

"So sorry, Backlash. Sounds like these people are here for the real star, Cody Curtis!"

The crowd thundered. Hops pumped his arms even harder, feeling alive. In the chute, someone stabilized Cody with a hand on his chest. Cody made the sign of the cross. Then Backlash twisted out, bucking hard.

Shutting off his microphone in case his foul mouth got the best of him, Hops ran toward the bull. Cody was a cowboy: born on a ranch, tossed off his first bronc at thirteen, expecting to end up gold buckle. He just had to hang on until the buzzer sounded. But with four seconds down, Cody was bouncing at a sliding left angle, trying to unsnag his glove.

Hops came at the bull sideways. Backlash eyed him between rotations, hairy nostrils flaring damp and angry, drool looping from his chin. Holding Backlash's gaze, Hops rushed him, close enough to brush his glove against the bull's thick waddle.

Cody used the distraction to crumple to the dirt. Hops hated those two seconds of side-eyed panic, praying his man wasn't taking a pounding to the skull. Something like that would be unforgivable, a mistake that would snuff out both their careers. As Hops flapped his arms, just about out of ideas, Cody's fringed figure climbed up and over the nearest gate.

In the middle of the arena, Backlash waited, now blinking and bored, like he'd already forgotten the past twenty seconds. When the gate opened, he sauntered back to the pens. The front rows laughed.

Hops strut across the dirt, relieved he hadn't screwed that up. "Gotcha," he laughed into the mic. He made certain his laugh sounded confident.

***

Cody raised a shot glass. "To Hops. The best man in the can." He had money signs in his eyes and victory in his sweat.

They ended their nights with Cuervo whenever Cody won, a tradition from their first run together in Missoula. As an only child, Hops had spent his childhood practicing knock-knock jokes on two border collies and his father's hogs. He'd never had a best friend, a fact that fell like the shadowside of a snow pine across his life. Then he clowned for Cody's first semi-pro ride two years ago. Cody had just moved to town to get serious about the Montana circuit and they fell in like brothers. Now Hops had a Facebook profile. Fourth of July cookout plans. Announcers calling him "Hops" instead of "clown." Some of Cody's shine, close enough to touch.

"Another win I can thank you for," Cody said.

Hops gripped his beer. Cody was the only one who recognized that these rides were a team effort. And that made Hops even more protective. "You had him the whole time."

"Can't do it without you, buddy. You're out there for what, twenty bulls a night? And I'm just sitting tight for eight seconds, hoping for the best."

"Gonna cry now?"

"Hell no am I letting a clown break me." Cody grinned. "I'm just saying those bulls are a planned car accident and you're my ambulance." He shook his head. "Fucking Kalispell."

Last year, a wily bull named Twister had dumped Cody after three quick seconds. A sloppy ride, it took a turn for the crazy when Twister charged Cody. Hops had cut in using his padded torso as a shield so Cody could clear the gate, but Hops got hooked by a horn and went airborne. Cody swung over just fine. Hops spent six days in surgery getting pieced back together, panicking about what he'd do if he couldn't get back to the dirt again. He never came up with an answer.

"Don't even with that," Hops said.

"I won't." Cody ordered another round of tequila. "But what I will do is get after you about coming with us. Bust out of Montana already."

"Here we go."

"And I'll keep going 'til I'm in the moving van, honking in your driveway." Cody had been pressuring him to move for months. But guys from all over the world—Canada, Brazil—swarmed Texas, trying for the big time. Those were the ones who landed the Ford sponsorships, not some tired old clown who worked the meat counter at Albertson's during the off-season. Hops imagined a life slinging pork loin full-time while Cody sat for interviews on ESPN.

"You've got a family, you're riding high on your game. I'm thirty-six. I head down to Texas and then what?" Hops sighed. "Better to be a new cowboy than an old clown."

"You'd be doing the same thing, just making more money," Cody said. "Been at this too damn long not to, so think about it." Cody raised his shot glass. "To something better."

As they slammed their glasses on the bar, a stocky blonde strolled toward them, her turquoise earrings swinging with each step. "Wrangler butts drive me nuts." She winked at Cody. "You thirsty, cowboy?"

"Nah," Cody said, holding up his half-full beer. "I'm taken, but Hops here's as free as the wind."

"And who doesn't like a good blow?" she said, grinning at Cody. "My name's Carleen."

Hops stared into his empty glass. Those ruddy cheeks, curls frizzing like baled hay: holy shit, Carleen Price, a face wilted by time, but one Hops remembered from tenth grade geometry. He'd had a crush on her all throughout high school. Never could muster the courage to ask her to prom. And here she was, eyes steely as buckshot, forehead creased like she'd spent years following the slow roll of wheat and acreage. Her sturdy thighs pushed out, bowlegged, her body curving as if it missed every second spent off the saddle. Something about her still looked good. Hops felt that old high school lump in his throat bubbling up like crude oil.

"I'm Cody and it's past my bedtime. But you're in good hands with Hops here, Montana's toughest bullfighter."

"Pleasure," Hops said.

"Hops, Carleen, enjoy the night. I'm heading home to my lady." With a brusque hug to Hops, he whispered, "Glove it before you shove it with that one."

Carleen finished off the dregs of his beer, her face stamped with the same disinterest she'd had while studying hypotenuses. She never drank in high school.

"So?" she asked, eyes fixed on the sixth inning of the Mariners game above the bar. "You clown?"

"Sure do." Hops wanted to grab her by the waist and ask her what she'd done since high school, when she'd left town, why she came back.

"You ever get hurt?"

He hoped a touch of mystery might make him more intriguing. "It's all been broken at some point."

"And you're buddies with Cody Curtis?"

"Best guy I know."

She turned to him, studying his face, a new flicker lighting her up. "How married is he?"

"Very," Hops said. Carleen was sitting close enough that he could smell the flowery scent of her hair. Maybe he could be big-time after all. "Not me though. I'm riding solo."

She downed the rest of his beer. "Good enough for me."

Hops winked and sucked in his gut.

***

The drive to his apartment took twenty minutes, about eight longer than Hops expected because he was driving slowly, trying hard to appear relaxed. Carleen's hand rested on his thigh, jostling closer to his belt buckle whenever he braked.

"Just the thought of you cowboys taming them bulls gets me all riled up," she said.

"I don't tame them. I distract them."

"Not like your buddy, huh?"

"Not at all," Hops said, pulling into the driveway. "You know, Carleen, we went to the same high school. Do you remember me?"

"Give me a hint."

"Sophomore year? We had geometry together. I was in the back row with the flat-top."

"No idea."

He wanted to take her to dinner sometime, buy her a nice rib eye and talk about her job, ask if she had any dogs. But it felt too late for formalities with her drunk and giggling just inches away from him on the porch while he rummaged for his key.

"That was years ago." She let her hands drift to his backside. "How's about making me buck right now, cowboy?"

"I'm not a cowboy."

When he opened the door, her hand yanked on his waistband, tugging his boxers down in the process. He stood there with half his ass hanging out, goosebumps prickling across the exposed skin.

"At least carry me over the threshold?" she asked.

"All right." He pulled up his pants and then bent to lift her.

She threw her head back and laughed. "Do I look like that kind of girl? Put me down." When she was standing on her own again, she pulled him close with one arm. "C'mere."

The pleasant weight of her breasts squashed against him, a sensation he hadn't felt in months. He'd never found anyone he was compatible with, opting instead for whoever was taking him home at last call.

Carleen rubbed on him. Two dry lips dragged across his face, followed by a stale wake of body odor. He tried kissing her slowly, but her mouth opened strangely wide. He prayed she wasn't yawning.

She fumbled with his fly and then slipped her hands into his underwear, giving him a clumsy squeeze. Hops winced, gently removing her wrists.

"Don't you like it rough, cowboy?" she asked.

"No."

"Kiss me."

"I'm trying to."

"C'mon, cowboy."

"I'm not a goddamn cowboy!"

Carleen sagged, drunk and angry, onto the couch. "Don't get all bent out of shape." She rolled her eyes. "Cowboy, high school, who cares?"

He'd spent so many teenage nights fantasizing about her, had refrained from explaining isosceles triangles in class so he wouldn't come off like a know-it-all. Now she was with him, and though it was different than he'd expected, to have her, almost twenty years past her prime, was still a win. She liked him, enough to come over. Hops grabbed her face with both hands. Lowering his lips to hers, he inhaled the sour tang of her breath, hoping her mouth would moisten with each kiss, maybe lose that smell.

"That's more like it," she said. Her tongue slopped over his face.

When it was over, missionary and quick, they laid on the carpet, panting. Hops could feel old carpet crumbs sticking to the sweat on his back.

MOUTH

"Well, yeehaw," she said with a slow clap when she stood. Using the recliner for balance, she pulled up her jeans. "Not bad."

"You don't have to leave, you know."

Carleen laughed. "Why bother? You'll clear out next week with the rest of them."

"Nah."

"Isn't Cody taking off?"

"Yeah. But I'm staying here."

"Why in hell would you do that?"

He shrugged. "If it ain't broke."

"I got an early morning colt start tomorrow." Carleen moved in a flurry of snaps and zippers. "Appreciate the offer, but I should keep it moving. Maybe you should too. Take care, clown." She blew him a kiss and shut the door.

Alone on the carpet, Hops curled his arms around his knees, the echo of her clap clanging like a fire alarm.

***

Gnats swarmed the floodlights on the final night of the season, the scents of hay, manure, popcorn choking the air. 4-H kids lined up around the pens to get a glimpse of the bulls. Or Cody. Under the bleachers, Hops tried to steady his nerves by stretching.

"Cowboy up, Hops!" Cody hollered as he walked over.

"I'm working on it. Ready for tonight?"

"Born ready." Cody wiped the sweat from his forehead. "You all right?"

"Just a little performance anxiety. Callie and the kid's up in the third row tonight." Cody gave Hops a once-over. "What's with this get-up?"

Hops avoided his gaze. "Not feeling my new look?"

Earlier in the day, Hops had distracted himself by messing around with his greasepaints. He'd normally coat his chin and eyes in white, outlines in black, add goofy details in red, yellow, blue. A wide smile and silly star eyes for the kiddos. But he'd gone with something new for the finals: pure yellow.

"You're brighter than the goddamn sun," Cody said, squinting at him.

"Aren't we big leagues? Figure I'd better dress the part."

"Do what now?"

"I'm heading to Texas." The lie came surprisingly easy. "Next week."

"Hell yeah," Cody shouted. "I knew you were better than this shitpit."

"All right, don't get a big head."

"What about Carleen?"

Hops had been scrolling through her photos on Facebook to find out where she trained horses, pinching and zooming on who she still hung out with from high school, keeping an eye out for her around town, hoping he'd catch her at the casino. "Once was plenty."

"Such a heartbreaker." Cody clapped him on the back.

Above the arena, the announcer's voice boomed. "Welcome, everyone, to the Big Sky Finals."

"Time to shine," Cody said. "Make it count."

"You got it." He prayed his voice didn't sound as rattled as he felt.

MOUTH

***

Hops paced until the stereo system piped in his polka intro. Then he ran into the arena doing the chicken dance, exaggerating five jumping jacks, dancing the twist.

"This is it, folks," the announcer said. It wasn't anyone Hops recognized. He gulped. Even their announcers were better. "Our championship cowboys are here for the finals and a chance to win ten thousand bucks. What do you say there, clown?"

Hops flinched. Then he spotted an orange helmet in the second chute. Cody smeared the bull rope with rosin, adjusting his position, smacking the bull's neck. Up in the third row, Callie was snapping photos while baby Colton squirmed on her lap. Hops, always a clown.

"I say it's go-time!" Hops yelled into his microphone, pumping his arms while the crowd roared. Though he'd lied to Cody about Texas, it was true he'd made a decision. Now he had to go through with it. And then live with it. What else could he do? Being big-time meant making tough calls. Hops felt the bitter burn of vomit rising, so he shut off his microphone.

"First up," the announcer said, "we got Beau Tanner."

Even in his boots, Beau was barely over five feet tall. Sometimes the little ones would hang tight until they died, sometimes they got flicked off like fleas.

"Hailing from Ronan, Beau has the pleasure of taking Voodoo out for his first ride tonight. Let's give it up for Beau."

Beau turned to wave to both sides of the arena, and with that, his eyes were off the prize, the ride already over. Hops scooted closer to the chute.

"Voodoo may be known for those crazy legs, but Beau, we got faith in you. Here we go."

The bull launched out of the chute, horns first, hips hinged. Belting across the dirt, Voodoo stretched into a full extension, his bell clanging.

Hops and Cooter skipped around, following each buck. After two seconds, Beau landed on his shins, as expected.

"Tough hit," the announcer said.

Duke cleared the bull back through his exit, while Hops jogged over to Beau and pulled him to standing.

"Shake it off," Hops said. "You got the next go-round." He hurried back out for Cody's ride.

"Next up is Montana's favorite cowboy, Cody Curtis!" the announcer wailed. Everyone strained toward the chute where the bull vaulted. "Trial by fire tonight, people. Cody's starting off with Undertow, a feisty eighteen-hundred pounds of jump and kick. Got plenty of try in this one."

Cody jerked back while he fiddled with his bull rope, Undertow thrashing beneath him. Hops spotted Colton pointing from his mother's lap, both of them chanting, *Daddy! Daddy!*

"Let 'er rip."

Undertow reeled out, a honey-colored slab of anger charging hard. Cody's helmet snapped off at three seconds, his free hand whipping sideways as his legs flopped loose. Hops waited.

"Boy, that bull's all twist and whip," the announcer said.

Cody slipped to the right inside the spin, then quickly spiraled down to the dirt, the rope wrapped around his hand.

"Not good, folks."

Cody was stuck in the well, Hops knew it, but still he held back, his terrible plan at full tilt now, pretending he couldn't get a good in as he waited out the bucks longer than any clown should. Two years of friendship. All those weekends spent trout fishing on the Bighorn, camping out like he was part of Cody's family, a family that invited him to every holiday, now clashed with his bullfighting instincts as he forced himself to stay put. The air smelled of night-cooled dirt and Montana, his home, the place where people were starting to like him. Nothing needed to change. Cooter and Duke sprinted toward Undertow while Hops lingered, hoping to appear cautious, possibly caught with a leg cramp. He'd never make it in Texas like his best friend would.

The bull whirled, hooves out. Duke dodged them. Cooter hollered and waved, his voice rasping, but Undertow stomped, nailing Cody. His upper thigh. A knee. Maybe his clavicle. Cody's arms snaked around his head, to protect it or keep it from spilling out, Hops wasn't sure.

It was all too much. Hops hadn't wanted it to get this far, he'd made it so much worse. He just wasn't good enough. Too old. Out of his league. And no amount of moving to a different state or trying harder would change that. Hops finally cut across. Undertow charged him, bucking off the rope, spittle coiling from his lips like a lasso loosened in the night air. Hops darted. As Cooter sprinted in from the left and Duke crossed from the right, Hops dove into his barrel.

"Just terrible," the announcer said. "Everyone hates to see that. Thankfully, we got Bill's excellent paramedic team on hand."

Hops waited inside the barrel, frantically considering ways to appear injured. He could hear the ambulance bouncing across the dirt, the gasps of a crowd that couldn't turn away. Still, he waited. Once he heard the exit chute clang, Hops climbed out of his barrel and stumbled toward Cody, exaggerating a limp.

Cody looked small. His shoulder was scrunched near his ear, his right leg folded like a chicken wing.

Hops grit his teeth as two paramedics eased Cody onto a stretcher.

"It's gone," Cody wheezed, his voice high, girlish. "All gone. I can't feel it."

"Try to breathe, Cody," a medic said. "We're getting you out of here."

Hops followed alongside them, wobbling.

"You ok, clown?" the other medic asked.

Hops waved him off. "I'll be fine."

"Then go tell Callie and Colton it ain't bad," the medic said. "Don't tell them nothing until you hear it from the doc first. And even then, you make it better than it is, you hear?"

Hops nodded, grimacing at Cody as the stretcher bounced. "Just stay with me, buddy. Please."

Cody howled. "Why me? Why?"

A paramedic slammed the doors and then tossed Cody's helmet to Hops. The ambulance sped out of the arena.

"How about a hand for our brave men?" the announcer asked.

The audience swelled into applause as Duke, Cooter, and Hops trudged to the middle of the arena. Hops stood, sweating as he clutched the helmet. It was dusty and dented and heavier than he expected. He took his bow.

A STEP AHEAD OF THE ALLIGATOR

Khakis pleated and apron starched, Rosemary tapped her feet at the bus stop, ready and now apparently delayed for her shift at the Cracker Barrel. Though she looked neat and felt crisp, even with this icky Jacksonville humidity, it'd be all for nothing if she waited any longer. Thirty-five years she'd been a Floridian—since she'd married Hudson—yet she still got overwhelmed by the intensity of summer. Like a pug panting in your face. It could ruin a whole morning's worth of Revlon. She kept a battery-powered fan in her pocketbook for this very reason, so she angled it toward the perspiration threatening to dribble down her neck.

"Can't I take you all the way in?" Hudson had asked ten minutes earlier from his recliner. "Let me be a gentleman on our anniversary."

"Don't be silly, sugar. That's not how you should spend today or your retirement." Rosemary hurried through the living room, switching off lights. "Besides, the bus will be here any minute."

"I'm bored. What am I supposed to do with myself all day?"

"You can start by turning off these lights. Such a waste to leave them on."

"Oh, the better to see you with," he said.

"What more could you possibly want to see?"

Now Rosemary was choking on a mouthful of sighs as she angled the fan around her face. When the bus arrived, four minutes late, she stepped on and lingered by the door, silently anticipating her reward. At sixty-four, she deserved a seat. The other riders pushed past her, so she wobbled a bit, just to make a point. Nothing. Glaring at the young men in the front seats, she gave a huffy sniff and shuffled toward the only open seat way in the back, squeezing next to a girl with a bedazzled cell phone at her ear.

The bus reeked of salami and feet. Rosemary brought her fingers under her nose and pretended to sneeze, inhaling the cocoa butter lotion she'd smeared on her hands since they, like her legs, could turn as scaly as one of Hudson's gators, her skin growing drier with each passing year. The smell of chocolate calmed her. Maybe she'd even treat herself to an éclair today. To heck with her waistband! She settled into her commute as she did each day: eyes forward, happy to be healthy, employed, and married to a real gentleman who'd honored his vows for thirty-five years.

"So hot," the girl next to her murmured.

Rosemary nodded. "It certainly is stifling."

When the girl didn't respond, Rosemary glanced over. She had the phone glued to her ear like everyone else.

"Let me hear you do it. Make it good."

Rosemary shifted in her seat, her shoe sticking to a wad of gum. She prayed it was gum.

"Nice and tight, huh? Where else can you put it?"

Rosemary's jaw unhinged. She twisted around, eager for the communal disgust. Yet no one cared. Was everyone a floozy these days? True, Rosemary used to neck with boys all the time during high school, but she kept things above the waist and over the clothes until she gave up her flower at nineteen. She'd certainly held onto that until she was in love. Granted, her first time wasn't with Hudson—that came a few years (and, if she was honest, two men) later—but Hudson was definitely her last.

Then the hussy purred. Out loud. Rosemary thought of Mittens, her grandmother's tomcat that had knocked up fifteen blocks worth of felines.

"Keep going."

Gasping, Rosemary leaned closer.

The girl giggled. "Just like the first time, huh?"

Rosemary aimed the fan toward her heaving cleavage, replaying that filth in her head.

***

Hudson glanced at his new watch. He had nine hours to himself, starting with the first pitch of the Marlins game. A whole afternoon of baseball and booze, just how retirement should be. Like getting to keep a cheeseburger delivered to the wrong table. All the time in the world had arrived and he had no idea what to do with it.

On his last day managing the gator processing plant five months ago, his crew had conspired to do the whole surprise party thing: a cooler of beers, some brisket, and the rest of the day off. Plus, the Timex. "So you remember to come home for dinner," they'd said. As if Rosemary hadn't been setting it out at six every single night for the last three decades.

"What's on deck for you after this?" his supervisor had asked.

Hudson didn't golf, wasn't big on boat repair. His closest buddies lived up north in cold towns he'd have to fly to. At sixty-five, he had hair shooting out of his ears. People called him sir these days, opened doors for him, spoke louder and slower. Every damn fool he met acting like an usher to his grave.

"I have no idea," Hudson had replied, feeling stale as soon as it came out of his mouth.

He lugged the Franzia from the refrigerator. A diehard beer guy, he never expected to get into white wine, of all things, during his retirement. Ladies drank Pinot Grigio. But when he'd been stationed in the Mediterranean during Vietnam, he learned a lot of things that surprised him.

The vino poured, he hunted for chips in the cupboard, scrounging up sunflower seeds instead. Great. Rosemary must be on one of her crackpot diets again. She'd get crazier than a bag of cats about those things. No sugar, only proteins, a jug of grapefruit juice mixed with some strange red pepper—whatever the fad, she always looked like regular old Rosemary, same as she had for the past thirty-five years. But, that's marriage: a blessing, a curse.

Raising the bag, he poured himself a mouthful. Rosemary tut-tutted whenever he did that, had a whole bellyaching routine about how he sounded like a piney rooter.

"Hudson, why do you go on like that?"

"I'm just being me."

"Then I must've married a real hog."

"Aw, give this piggy a kiss."

"Not like that," she'd say, shooing him away.

He let the bag rest against his lips. If he wanted anything more, he could fry up one of his gator steaks. Hell, he could stuff himself with anything he wanted now and she wouldn't find out. Something soothing in the ease of retirement, like he was a bachelor.

***

"Rise and shine, Cracker Barrel team."

Rosemary perched in her usual spot, center front with a clipboard, for their weekly employee meeting. As usual, the staff could probably benefit from a cold Sprite and three more hours of sleep. But it was already nine in the morning. Another Tuesday night spent whooping it up like responsibility was for dopes. Oh she'd seen the billboards for Bud Light, she knew the skimpy numbers girls wore these days. They'd stay single forever if they kept that up. She gave the laminated seating chart a spritz. The smell of clean reassured her everything was in order.

Her manager, Ed, was younger than her, probably about forty, the remaining strands of his hair shrinking from his head like half-done bacon. With quite the belly making his shirt buttons strain. Rosemary smirked. Hudson had maintained a military physique all these years. Yes, he talked less than when they were first married, especially during baseball season. And football. And now NASCAR too. But he kept the leanness she loved: the thatched tendons of his legs, those strong knobby fingers, all the soft white hairs curling out from his chest.

Like any wife, she craved a little sugar, some sweetness to take them both to those furtive nights out back under her mother's oak tree. Such a long time ago. She wished she had the confidence, or the tan, to be nude in front of him. It'd been years, something that had just stopped as if they forgot to pay the water bill. He never did anything about it anymore, didn't even get handsy on his birthday or Valentine's Day. Must be normal. Hudson was retired now and should be more interested in his James Patterson stories. They were probably too old for it anyway.

"We all here?" Ed gripped his travel mug of coffee. Then, as if there were no ladies present, he shoved an onion-smeared sausage link into his mouth. She cleared her throat to get him to stop. He took another bite, the mustard splattering on his paunch.

"Rooster's missing," one of the dishwashers yelled.

Ed rubbed his temples.

"I'll go find him," Rosemary sighed.

"I'd lose my dang head if it weren't for you, Rosemary."

She imagined him on a guillotine and smiled.

***

Hudson squinted at their living room wall, pinned with thirty-five years of photos. That muggy wedding day at the courthouse, him sweating through his best button-down, Rosemary dabbing not her eyes, but her upper lip, a sharp chemical smell where the blonde down had been quickly removed. Their honeymoon in Tucson. The tenth annual family reunion in the park, then the fifteenth, Hudson and Rosemary the only couple who never ended up with kids doing cannonballs in the pool. They'd tried to make a baby, had focused on it for ten years until it just wasn't fun anymore. Neither of them wanted to know whose fault it was, so they never went to a doctor. But Rosemary didn't let him touch her much after that. He missed it.

Hudson reached inside the desk drawer for his stack of photos. Vietnam. His buddies, their combat packs, posed among the sun-bleached history of Italy. They were kids. Unprepared for the silence commemorating their return, that nagging chill of respect, shame. All those stupid nicknames, the secrets. But still, a future shimmering like the ocean, wide and free. The siren song of adventures yet to come. He studied their faces. It'd been the best time of their lives. When Hudson caught his reflection in the mirror, a face like a rusted anchor, he realized he'd been crying.

***

Rosemary zipped through the restaurant, noting she was pretty fit for being the granny on the team. Well, technically she had no grandbabies. Did that just make her an old lady? She chose not to think about it. Instead, Rosemary did a lap through the Old Country Store.

Crammed with vintage farm equipment and cookware, the store stretched like one giant yard sale. No, even better—like the set of *Antiques Roadshow*. Such a pleasure knowing those old fixtures got a new purpose.

"Rooster?" she called.

Rosemary dawdled by the bags of Maple Nut Goodies, pulled her hand back. She had to keep her focus. She'd once caught him paw-deep in the saltwater taffy bin. He'd laughed when he saw her, swallowed a last piece, and slid his hand from the candy. She never said a word about it to anyone. Maybe people can change if you just let them.

Rooster wasn't there or on the grill, so she pushed through the battered kitchen door. Outside, the morning tossed itself on her like a damp wool blanket. Traffic roared, swirling with the sweet stink of diesel, spoiled catfish, turnip greens. Rosemary pinched her nose. Rooster had a nasty Kool habit that often took him out back to light up. Boy, did she want to rip into him for letting something so dirty take over his life. He even rolled his own cigarettes, like a bum. She scanned the boxes and buckets, the tangle of broken rocking chairs. And then, just as she suspected, Rosemary spotted Rooster's spiky hair. She strode toward him.

"Where you been?" she yelled, the wake of a passing big rig muffling her shouts.

Rooster leaned against the graffitied trash bin, his eyes shut.

"Hey! Been trying to find you."

He gripped the bin's edge, and while those strong biceps pulsated, a blonde head bobbed at his waist.

Rosemary clutched a box flap, standing there long enough for her lip gloss to evaporate. She was still standing there when Rooster opened his eyes and winked.

***

In truth, Hudson had joined the Navy because he was staring down the draft. He wasn't some pussy draft dodger, though. He just didn't want to die in Vietnam like his older brother Jack, a Marine, scared it would be his boot to slip on a banana leaf and tap the landmine that'd launch his whole squad into the bright blue sky. So he signed up for the floating life. When he got assigned to a ship off of Italy, he felt relieved he wouldn't face combat. When he broke it off with Rosemary the night before his deployment, he figured he was doing the right thing.

"Don't cry," he'd said. "It's just something I've got to do."

"I'll wait for you," Rosemary said.

"I can't promise anything."

"You don't have to."

Six months before the end of his tour felt like a good time to answer her stack of letters. He had acted like a young man at sea. It was time to settle down.

When Hudson walked off the destroyer and across the parking lot, Rosemary had been sweating for an hour in her white linen dress, standing in the shade by the gas station bathroom with a fistful of irises. The veil hung in the backseat of her car, just like they'd planned.

***

"Ketchup bottles," Ed was saying. "Keep 'em clean. Guests hate grabbing at them when they're all sticky with someone else's gunk."

Rosemary returned to her seat, almost sliding right off it. Sweat shot down her back, her underclothes damp.

"Any luck?" Ed asked.

Moist. She felt inappropriately moist.

"Ah, our new server." Ed glanced over Rosemary's head. "Everyone, meet Sunny. Today's her very first day."

Southern ladies get away with fake smiles better than anyone else and Rosemary aimed to work hers all the way out. She turned around and grinned at the whore.

***

In the garage, Hudson tore through beach chairs and tarnished barbeque equipment, keeping an eye out for water moccasins as he foraged for his rucksack. He was already starting to feel young and free.

Once he found the bag, flattened and reeking of raccoon urine, it only took him ten seconds to pound the silverfish away with a broom, swing the pack onto his shoulders, and know he wanted that old rush back.

Hudson dragged it into the bedroom and began stuffing it with his shirts and pants.

***

Were they even dating? Or did that tramp open wide for any old joe? And with her mouth? Rosemary gently gnawed on her knuckle. Early in their romance, Hudson had often asked Rosemary for that very thing, had even gently pushed her head down there once, but she could never bring herself to do it. She had not been raised to get on her knees for a man. And how unsanitary: after a sticky summer day, his privates must smell worse than an armpit. Hers certainly had an evening aroma, which is also why she hid her laundry. No need for him to be poking around with the slight white remnants of each day smudged inside her panties, right there in plain sight. He didn't need to know everything.

And yet, Rooster's grin. She blushed, imagining Hudson smiling just like that.

MOUTH

***

Three decades with one woman.

"To the only ham sandwich you'll ever eat again," his buddies had slurred at his bachelor party. At the time, it hadn't scared him. If he could figure out war, he could figure out marriage. Besides, half of those boneheads had gotten divorced.

Hudson gripped the pen. He should leave a note out of respect. And to keep her from reporting the car as stolen. A few years ago, riled up after one of their arguments (her jealous ways, him blowing the bank on fishing equipment), Hudson had imagined the complaints he'd scrawl out on the notepad they used to make grocery lists:

1. You sleep too close to me in bed.

2. Except for your fried chicken, you never cook with enough salt.

3. I've visited a strip club five times during our marriage.

It had been thirty-five years of yes dear-ing, six long ones without her touch. But a letter she could unfold over and over? And on their anniversary? That was cruel. Instead, he left a lamp on in the living room, willing the brightness to whisper what he couldn't.

***

Twenty minutes before the end of her shift, Rosemary strode into the kitchen. A debutante is forever—she would handle herself with grace and class.

"Got lots of compliments on your catfish tonight," Rosemary said to Rooster across the pick-up counter. Her voice sounded controlled. She smeared apple butter on a biscuit.

"Is that the word?" Rooster asked.

"Sure enough."

"See something you like out there today?"

"Beg your pardon?"

Rooster grinned. "Bet you would beg. Maybe get on your hands and knees, bark like a junkyard dog."

Rosemary grew sweaty and dizzy. "Shut your mouth right now, Rooster. I saw you out there acting like a pig. At least I can sleep knowing I never have to get on my knees for any man." She smelled Sunny approaching, so she stretched an alligator smile across her face.

"Hello, ma'am," Sunny said.

Rosemary nodded, steadying herself with another biscuit.

"Table ten said those the best chops they ever put in their mouth, Rooster." As Sunny reached across Rosemary to grab a catfish sandwich, she accidentally knocked Rosemary's elbow. Biscuit chunks cascaded down Rosemary's shirt, leaving her upper lip mustached with butter.

Sunny blushed. "Oh, I made a mess of you. I'm sorry."

Rosemary brushed that tasty biscuit off her apron. "A good reminder to keep our eyes open to what's going on around us."

As Sunny bent down to scoop the crumbs, her perfume swelled, cheap and overpowering.

"Sunny," Rosemary said, "I've just got to know. What is that scent you got on?"

Rooster hollered.

Sunny's eyes flashed like two lightning bugs. "It's Jovan Musk."

"It's perfect."

"Thank you, ma'am. You should give it a whirl. Might find you really love it."

Rosemary bit into a new biscuit.

***

Hudson sped through their neighborhood. Thirty-five years. It wasn't that he didn't love Rosemary. He did and had never once dipped the wick during their marriage, not even ten years ago when Lana used to garden in her shorty shorts next door and they could've easily made it happen in the garage while Rosemary was at the salon. He'd thought about it, that's for sure, imagined what Lana would smell like behind her ears, how those crimson nails would feel dragging between his shoulder blades. For months they'd flirted over the cocoplum hedge, joking about the latest perennial she was killing or the longest gator he'd stripped.

One Saturday, Lana stood on his porch with a UPS slip in her hands. "This came to me by accident." She wore a yellow halter top and tight denim skirt. "I'd bring it over myself, but I can't carry it."

Hudson shut the door quickly so Rosemary wouldn't call after him. "You lead the way."

As they crossed her lawn, the sprinkler sprayed their legs. They darted through the water, both of them laughing.

"I haven't done that in years."

Lana giggled. In her air-conditioned foyer, she shut the door behind them. "Best to keep the cool in and the gators out."

The package contained a spinning rack for all his fishing rods and was probably light enough that he could carry it on his own. Lana bent over, her titties stretching the hell out of that halter top as she maneuvered the box.

"Watch your back, there." He placed his hand against her damp skin, the scent of suntan oil heavy in the air. He'd spent the day salting gator hides and prayed he didn't smell fusty.

"Looks like you've got it under control."

"What if we head upstairs and get out of control?" He hadn't expected to say anything and was both surprised and excited when his words poured out like sweet tea.

Lana took his hand and Hudson followed her upstairs, her palm warmer, softer than Rosemary's. As soon as the comparison flashed through his mind, Hudson felt sick. He climbed the stairs. A house just like his.

She obviously lived alone: orange lingerie tossed on the floor, a half-eaten caramel on the nightstand. "I've been hoping for this since I moved in." Lana leaned back on the bed, her legs smooth and shiny. She tugged at her halter, exposing the bright white triangle of her tan line and one hard nipple. "What do you think?"

Gently, Hudson squeezed the soft curve of her breast. She moaned, tipping her head back, and with his fingers on the warm underside of her softness, Hudson thought of how Rosemary had trembled under the oak tree the night before his deployment. She said she'd never been so happy or so sad, something he'd never understood. Until now.

"It's okay," Lana said.

MOUTH

Hudson opened his eyes. "What?"

"I can fix it." She worked harder on him. "Just relax."

He shut his eyes tight and tried, but Rosemary's face misted through his thoughts like morning steam off the swamp. All those years. The woman who'd held him on the kitchen floor after his father died in that boating accident, the woman who'd made him key lime pie for his birthday every year because it was his favorite as a kid. And what would he do after this? Leave her? Lana tightened her perfect grip. He had to lie to one of them. Lana was smiling up at him.

"You're not doing it right."

She looked surprised. "Then tell me how you'd like it."

"I can't." Yanking his hand away, Hudson pushed himself off her bed. He moved quickly to beat back the regret hissing in his ears.

"C'mon, Hudson. It's not too late."

But he was already zipping his pants, smoothing his T-shirt, planning to tell Rosemary the package must've gotten lost in the mail. He avoided Lana's eyes so he could finish out the lie. "It's just not what I was hoping for is all."

"Me neither. But you didn't even give it a chance."

Hudson felt small and trapped. He shrugged.

"If you leave, you can never come back here," she said. "You got that?"

He bounded down the stairs and then bolted out of Lana's front door, running through her sprinklers back to his yellowed lawn. As soon as he got home, Hudson licked the fingers that had touched her. They'd tasted salty.

***

Rosemary dashed off the bus three streets before her usual stop, the summer air as thick as spilled syrup. She couldn't believe herself, wheezing across the Save-Mart parking lot.

Although she loved a bargain, Rosemary never lowered herself to Save-Mart, of all places. And she didn't feel bad about that. She wasn't exactly sure when society had deemed it acceptable to wear a bikini top while shopping (in public!), but Save-Mart was apparently the place to let it all hang out. Unfortunately, it was also the only store open, and closing in five minutes, so she tore down the aisles, scanning for the perfumes. Jovan Musk was on the lowest shelf. Figures.

On the way to pay, she passed an underwear display. Several satin numbers covered the table, right there where everyone walked by. Panties weren't even private anymore. She pretended to rummage through some nearby cotton nightgowns, glancing around in case anyone saw her. When she verified she was indeed alone, she grabbed the last size L-Grande panties off the display.

Rosemary headed toward the oldest cashier in the store, figuring her eyes would be too weak to judge the purchase.

"Hi, dear," the cashier said.

"Good evening, ma'am."

"Still hotter than Hades out there?"

"Yes, it's quite warm."

"Do you need some lube to go with these?"

"I'm sorry?"

"Personal lubricant. More slip for your slide."

"I beg your pardon."

MOUTH

The cashier folded the panties. "We older gals often need that oomph. You know, water the grass to make the house look nice." She winked.

"I am nowhere near as old as you."

She chuckled. "All I know is lube saved my marriage to hubby number four. I feel bad for the other three fellas. Must've been like humping a mound of sand." She handed everything to Rosemary in a plastic bag. "Anywho, have fun, dear."

"Screw you," Rosemary hissed and bounded through the door.

***

Hudson opened up his Chrysler on I-95, the speedometer twitching shy of ninety while he switched lanes, weaving between cars to nail the spot with the most open asphalt. The rev, the hot feel of life, of choice, all at his control. But even with the windows down, it wasn't enough. He wanted the spray of water. Cool winds. Cranking the air conditioner on high, Hudson angled the vents so the air would hit him right in the face. More. He widened his mouth and tried to swallow, his breath hurricaning from his dry parted lips. Hudson thought of Italy. Lana's smell. What his next three hundred afternoons would look like. He punched the accelerator.

***

"Happy anniversary, honey," Rosemary called into the house.

Though the car was gone, the living room lamp was on. And at the brightest setting, too. Typical. Hudson probably ran out for more potato chips. The man craved salt like a deer.

Maybe he was even picking up irises for her like he did every year on their anniversary.

As Rosemary reached under the lampshade to turn off the light, her fingertip brushed the hot bulb and snapped back. How Hudson hadn't burned their house down was a daily miracle.

She shuffled through the familiar darkness of their home.

***

Parked on the highway shoulder fifty miles from home, Hudson sat in the car. One perfect titty.

He spit in his palm and unbuckled his pants, the car rocking, and as he leaned back, far, farther, the memory exploded. His adrenaline faded into a long, slow flatline, the daily tempo of his life.

Hudson shook his hand out the window, flinging the memory from his fingertips.

***

Rosemary clasped the pair of sateen panties. They were crimson and smooth with a pearl dangling from the top. Cool to the touch. She hugged them to her night-damp chest. Cheap, but maybe he'd like that. She had let all those years of lingerie opportunities pass, when her hips hourglassed and Hudson couldn't stop grabbing at her. What a waste. These days, she felt like a white elephant gift wrapped in the Sunday funnies.

She slid on the new panties, crumpling her usual flowered cotton briefs into the trash can. The new ones came up quite high in the back, enough that she had to tug them down and out. She wondered if Sunny had that problem. Her rear was half the size of Rosemary's and jutted out like a walnut waiting to be cracked.

Then she spritzed the Jovan Musk on her neck, the crooks of her arms, behind both knees. Every lady has her own spray pattern, a secret code of aerial seduction, and though Rosemary hadn't worn perfume in years, she remembered the spot that Hudson liked best: right behind her ears. With the musk floating through the room, she climbed across their bed.

On the sheets, hands splayed in front of her, Rosemary knelt. She stretched into position, hips pushing back. It wasn't so bad. Rosemary adjusted her body, sucked in her stomach. She would wait for him to arrive, would pose that way on their bed until he came home. Just like the first time.

***

The floorboards creaked as Hudson entered the foyer. Their home, the dusty scent of their bodies. He dropped his keys in the clamshell dish and, out of habit, turned to the pantry for a snack.

Hudson funneled sunflower seeds into his mouth, but they tasted stale. He filled a mason jar with water and arranged the irises inside.

He'd been driving for hours and now, starving, he opened the freezer. A gator steak slid from the shelf, cold and quick. He jumped to the right but it nailed his foot, clattering on the kitchen floor. Hudson waited for Rosemary to yell, for the stinging to stop. When neither happened, he shoved the meat back into the freezer, a tangle of curses under his tongue.

He limped down the hall, a hall like all the others on the block, a hall he'd walked down a thousand times. In their bedroom, his wife slept, knees curled, arms blotchy, a crocheted blanket over her hips. She didn't normally sleep like that. He fumbled toward his side of the bed, foot throbbing as he lay down, a scent of soured sugar lingering in the room.

"Where'd you go?" Rosemary murmured.

"Not far," he whispered, settling into the cool white sheets. He kissed her hand. "I'm back."

CLIMATE CHANGE

SATURDAY, JUNE 14

When you were little, a Saturday outing to the zoo usually clocked in at two excruciating hours in the station wagon. But today, with you strapped in an ambulance, it's a four-hour ordeal.

"Is it nice out?" you ask from the stretcher.

"Just about there," Eustace, your wife, calls from the front seat.

The ambulance strains up the long driveway, past the zoo, to the backlot of the animal hospital. This is the second time Dr. Ramirez has sent you here to be weighed since his office scales max out at 300 pounds. You imagine all four Goodyears popping like round-nose bullets.

"And no polar bears today, right?"

"I promise," Eustace says. "Just in and out. Then we'll celebrate the good news."

Last month, while flipping through the mail, you noticed a flyer from the World Wildlife Fund. On it, a polar bear clung to a meager ice chunk under the headline: *My home is melting*. That damn bear is all you think about these days.

The ambulance doors bang open with blistering sunshine, a harsh reminder that you can't handle any wattage stronger than the bulbs in your living room. You used to be the guy sporting brand-new Oakleys every summer, an expert boatsman dodging mosquito squalls on the annual bass-fishing trip. But you haven't walked unassisted since the accident two years ago. At your last weigh-in, you'd tottered in at 507 pounds.

Six paramedics shuffle into position: one at your head, two gripping either side of the stretcher, one avoiding the split skin on the soles of your feet, and two more anxious outside the doors in case you torpedo forward. You feel bad for them, pinioned to the Missouri humidity by your giant body.

"Ready?" They squat as low as adult men can. "Lift."

If you haven't lost seventy-five pounds by now, Dr. Ramirez can't sign off on your gastric bypass next week. And you're serious about dropping the 174 pounds you've packed on since getting T-boned. Sure, you were never a thin guy—your passion for crispy snoots certainly guaranteed that—but back then, your weight was a big-boned 238.

Still, it was surprisingly easy to get this huge. The first fifty pounds settled in when you were laid up in the hospital bed the doctor had installed in the living room. For six slow months, you were prostrate in front of the TV, waiting for your femur, your pelvis, part of your clavicle to set, sutures to heal, a listless process that left you doughy and reeking. And that was fine—you and Eustace were so grateful you hadn't died, you'd even clasped hands with the weird hospital chaplain and prayed together.

But by the time Dr. Ramirez approved your bed exercises, guilt was already contaminating you and Eustace. With you bedridden and unable to work, she shouldered all the grocery shopping and cooking, the housecleaning, the never-ending medication pick-ups, the car insurance and medical bill battles. You had become accustomed to your new supine lifestyle, whiling away the boredom with pre-made snacks from grocery outlets, cheap treats that kept you distracted while she fretted about your daily care. Eventually, your mouth just grew used to the sense of duty and accomplishment associated with finishing a box of chocolate Krispy Kremes, the ease of dunking tortilla chips in queso fundido, all the wonderful foods you could balance on your chest between bites. Before you knew it, you needed two male nurses under your shoulders in order to stand up. The rest of the weight simply piled on, something you hardly noticed, like Parmesan melting on spaghetti.

"Grab it," the guy near your head says. But it's too late. The sheet across your waist slips away and exposes the crusty lymphedema on your left shin, as pitted as a moldy orange peel.

Eustace yanks the sheet back over your waist. "Don't worry about them," she whispers to you.

Ron and the other veterinary technicians have already propped open both doors for your gurney. At least they're not snickering like that jerk from your first weigh-in.

"Hi Ron," you say. "This better be the last time we meet."

"Hope so too, pal."

A shriek—from a rhino? a gorilla?—swells down the hall as they wheel you into the cool concrete room. Half of it is caged off with those stalls you saw on field trips to the farm, while a scratched steel scale dominates the rest. It reeks of stomped grass and hooves. Over the past three months, you've been vigilant about your exercises, rolling your legs inward to remind your quads they have a purpose, pointing and flexing your toes to reinvigorate your dissolved calf muscles. You're lighter, you can feel it.

"All right, load him up."

An acrid undercurrent eddies toward the scale, along with the stinging realization that you haven't had a bowel movement this week, even though you've been choking down bowls of steamed spinach during dinner. Is this one more diabetes complication? Entire afternoons have been lost scouring the internet about dialysis and blindness and amputation. Without the surgery, you'll be fused to that bed forever.

"Eustace!"

"What, honey?"

At thirty-seven, she's way too young to be caught in the crossfire of obligation and frustration, but she's become quite knowledgeable about the contents of your bedpan, swabbing washcloths between your layers and smelling fungal odors that no amount of Nystatin can cover up, her face appearing more pummeled each month. If only you could treat her to a cruise in the Bahamas to thank her for stepping into this role of caregiver forty years too early. Eustace would love doing her crosswords on the sand, taking breaks to paddleboard across the aquamarine waves, her hair streaked with blonde. But if she goes on vacation, there won't be anyone to wash you.

"Will you hold my hand?" you ask.

She pats your wrist and crosses her fingers. "Four thirty-two."

Should you ask about getting to a toilet? You imagine having to squat over an outdoor pit, same as the elephants. But now you're on the scale and the technicians have stepped away, leaving you heaped in front of everyone, anxious and tangled in your white sheets like a fallen emperor. The numbers fly: 193, 247, 313.

"Good drive up?" Ron asks.

MOUTH

"Slow." Your stomach gurgles. All these people as witness. One of them could easily put this on YouTube.

"June's been hotter than blazes this year."

Sweat pours down from your armpits. "Never felt one like this before."

"Praying it doesn't keep up. Can't imagine we'd make it through." Ron studies the scale. "Okay, we're at four twenty-one."

Exhaling, you pump your fist and then realize that shrieking sound is not a hyena, but your wife weeping as she delivers hugs to everyone around you.

***

SUNDAY, JUNE 15

The surgery date is now on the kitchen calendar lassoed in red ink: Thursday, June 19. In just four days, at eleven in the morning, Dr. Ramirez will partition off the worst part of you. For now, though, it's time to make up for the two years spent acting like the whole world was your trough. You've promised Eustace that you'll be good—all dino kale, fourteen glasses of water, no more Squirt—but it's hard monitoring every single thing that goes down the hatch. What about celebrating the time you broke off one corner of the butter cake instead of eating the entire pan? People discount your brain because of your girth. But tonight, you'll prove you've changed. With Eustace out running errands, you maneuver toward the kitchen on your mobility scooter. Nailed above the entryway is your prized possession: the mount of a fifty-nine pound flathead you'd caught night fishing at the river three years ago. Mud-colored with whiskers six inches long, the catfish gapes from the wall, the shock of being caught imprinted in his expression. Never before have you felt so proud of yourself, so strong. You named him Steve.

"Things are changing around here, Steve-O," you say as you motor under him. "Wait 'til you get a load of the new me."

In the kitchen, you peer at the chicken you've been roasting, the carrots and onions and sweet potatoes bubbling in the pan. You take it out and grab a stick of margarine from the refrigerator, smearing the bird so it gleams. That'll keep the juices in tight. But maybe you should check to make sure. You run your finger along its heat-crinkled skin and can't help but twist off a greasy piece.

"Don't tell anyone," you warn him.

Salt and melted butter—a comfort so primal that you stuff the chicken skin even deeper in your mouth, your knuckles knocking against your wisdom teeth, filling yourself so air can't ruin the ecstasy of this moment.

Maybe just one more bite, you think, and keep thinking, until the whole chicken is stripped to the pale white meat.

***

Eustace returns home and eyes the kitchen table: two goblets of cucumber water, a bowl of carrots, paper towels folded like fans. "What's all this?"

"Something to thank you for taking care of me."

She wraps her arms around your neck, avoiding the hump that's developed on your upper back. It's the first time she's hugged you in months. "And you took the skin off. I'm so proud of you."

"Thanks." Flushed, you carve the chicken.

She pours vinaigrette over her spinach salad, not even bothering to ration out her serving. "Maybe this is a good time to tell you I've been thinking of something important, too."

"Oh yeah? Are you extending your family leave?"

"No. But I stopped off at the disability office today."

"How come?"

"It's been two years—you know my leave runs out soon. But now that the surgery's happening, I'll be able to return to work."

"You want to go back?"

"Of course. Don't you?"

Thinking back to your thirteen-hour days bent over in the sun as a cement mason, you realize you don't miss it at all.

She forks a tomato. "I think we should start interviewing nurses for you."

"But you already take care of me. No one else will know how to do it right." Before the accident, Eustace worked as a neonatal intensive care nurse and you rarely had Date Night. After her usual Wednesday night happy hours, she'd come home with salacious stories about which doctors were hooking up, which nurses were bulimic. This whole life outside you. Having her home has made things less lonely.

"We need the money. And the insurance," she says.

"We can talk about it."

"I set up two interviews for tomorrow afternoon."

A White Castle Crave Case is the only thing that could calm you right now. "This is way too soon, Eustace. I can't believe you're doing this to me."

Eustace stops eating and stares you down. "Really? Are we going to play that game?"

"You tell me."

She flings her napkin on top of her dinner. "Eat your carrots."

***

MONDAY, JUNE 16

It's too hot to sleep. Dinner was a bust, leaving things awkward with Eustace. And you've been up since then, fixating on worst-case scenarios: Eustace stepping out with one of the young ortho fellows. Or her slipping up after Trivia Night with some lounge act in from Branson for the weekend. Losing her would hurt worse than getting T-boned, so you distract yourself by brainstorming ways to apologize.

Since the accident, Eustace has been sleeping on the couch next to your bed in the living room. Maybe, if you scooch to the side of the bed and nudge her, she'll want to do it. It's been two years since you've been naked together, your longest dry spell yet. "We'd estimate a year recovery, but it could take longer," the doctors had said. And so, for the first time in your relationship, you both abstained.

Throughout these tough times, Eustace has maintained her skinny figure. In fact, she's never weighed more than 132 pounds throughout your entire marriage. It's a discipline you should admire. But honestly, it's irritating that she can inhale an entire order of toasted ravioli whenever she wants.

Other than that, though, you've been going through this together, each of you feeling cooped up and dealing with the midday crankies, avoiding chocolate, clipping new recipes that use quinoa. She hasn't had any extra time for her girlfriends or Zumba or getting her hair cut, which is even longer than normal now and cascades unruly down her back. It's sexy on her. She's come through for you during this ordeal, despite everything. But what happens to you when she's back out there?

Stretching as far as you can, forearm aching with the effort, you poke her shoulder and then rest your palm against the cool bars of your bed.

"Eustace?"

In sickness and in health, you'd whispered under the ivy trellis at your wedding. But after the accident and all the weight gain, things looked and smelled different. Like the chapped apron of skin she'll have to raise with her forearm in order to dig out your erection.

"Sweetie?"

Jolting awake, she reaches for the bedpan.

"No, I don't need to go," you say.

She falls back on her pillow. "Did you have a nightmare?"

"Yes." Able to reach her arm now, you rub the smooth divot of her elbow. "Know any way to fix it?"

She pauses. "I'm still pissed about what you said."

"I know, but maybe I can make it up to you. Besides, when was the last time we did it?" You know exactly when: three days before the accident, on the couch, during the fourth inning of the Cardinals game.

Her uncertainty hangs like a meat hook. "I don't know. It's been so long."

"I think I can do it if you help me."

"But I put lotion on my hands."

"Can you wash your hands?"

She sighs. "Hold on."

While you wait, you pray everything down there will cooperate. And smell okay.

Eustace returns and kneels at your side. She didn't use any mouthwash, but you push past the gluey stink, inching your fingers into her long brown hair, twisting the strands around your fingers. You shift your hand down and press against the front of her pajama bottoms. She's never been so quiet, but you remember some of the moves she likes, the muscle memory of married pleasure, and, after a while, she pulls down her pants. She's apparently stopped shaving. How long has that been going on?

You peek, terrified she's pretending, but her eyes are shut and you pray she's envisioning Johnny Depp instead of her jiggling blob of a husband. This infidelity makes you soften, but your hardworking, patient wife deserves the fantasy. Eustace tugs harder. Imagine yourself mustachioed, captain of a galleon you've overtaken, her perfect C-cups cresting in a corset dress. You paw inside her Wells Fargo T-shirt. She moans a bit, hopefully not just for show, and leans to lift the apron of your stomach.

"Am I hurting you?" she asks.

"No, but can you get your knee off my stomach?"

"Sorry."

"And careful with my bad leg."

She's really dry, so she spits in her hand before mashing you in, and then you're Johnny Depp again, a pirate, a bad boy, tan, ripped, it's you she wants, you, your heart could just burst, and then you do.

"I'm back, huh?" you wheeze.

Eustace pecks you on the cheek before hurrying to the shower, the moment a thin dribble down her thigh.

***

You are giddy. Sure, the sex this morning lacked the sizzle you two used to have, but it's a good reminder of the man who once went downtown on her in the mudroom during the neighborhood ugly Christmas sweater party. He's still in there.

Now, with just three hours before the interviews, you're back on track pointing and flexing your toes the requisite thirty times during *Maury*. He's of course preparing to announce paternity results. One woman, one cross-eyed baby, five potential fathers. Two of them are brothers. Isn't it like announcing to the whole world that you're a big slut? Shows like this elate you, the reassurance that there are people worse off than you. But they also scare you. One of your greatest fears is that Eustace will surprise you with a film crew to shame you into losing weight on live TV.

A girl, seventeen, wails as she discovers the young man hopping across the set is not her daughter's father.

"It's okay," she sobs. "I have ideas about who it could be."

"I'm heading out for a quick errand," Eustace says. "You good here?"

"Yeah." You smile at her, admiring her backside as she passes. "This morning was good too."

She inclines her head in a way you can't decipher, grabs the car keys. "I'll be home for the interviews."

"Don't rush," you say, glancing past her to ensure there isn't a boom or tripod outside.

And then you're all alone. In the crushing silence that follows, you consider the entry table photos: a black and white wedding shot of you dipping her on the dance floor. You weighed 224 on your wedding day. Another one, Eustace laughing in waders as she helps you hold Steve. You stare at his smooth yellowed skin, the clear, round eyes, remembering how proud you'd felt hoisting him up in front of everyone at the dock. In fact, you stare for so long, you almost don't realize Eustace has driven off without her trademark double honk.

***

With fifteen minutes before the first interview and Eustace still not home, you settle into your afternoon TV lineup, confident she must've come to her senses and canceled the meetings.

"Hi honey," she says, hurrying in from the back door. She's got a bounce in her step and a cropped hairdo. The curls are gone, all of them. Her hair barely skims her ears.

You mute the TV. "What have you done?"

"I needed a fresh start."

"It's awful."

"I like it." She fusses with it in the mirror, pinching strands so they cup her excellent cheekbones. "Feels more like me."

"If you were a totally different person."

"You'll get used to it." The doorbell rings and she peeks through the front windows. "The first guy is here. Can you please be nice?"

You snap the sheets tighter around your body and focus on Steve.

Eustace returns with a young man—shaved head, at least two mermaid tats, arms like fire hydrants.

"Hey," he says, waving from the doorway. "I'm Brian."

"Brian, you're certainly jacked," you say. "How much can you bench?"

"Thanks. Probably about one twenty."

"So, with me at over four hundred pounds, there'd be no way to help if I fell?"

Brian glances at Eustace. "Well, I was under the impression that the position is for a bed-bound patient?"

"If you do your job right, I won't be forever."

Eustace blushes. "I'm sorry, Brian. What my husband is trying to say is that—"

"Wait a second. If Brian here doesn't understand English, we have a bigger problem."

"I clearly understand English, sir, but—"

"You're just dumb then?"

Brian stands to shake Eustace's hand. "Ma'am, I'm sorry, but this isn't the right fit for me."

You smile. One down.

"Let me walk you out," she says. When Brian reaches the living room, her voice drops. "It's just that my husband's in a tough spot and extra vulnerable right now."

"I'm fat," you yell, "but my ears aren't. Stop talking about me like I don't exist."

The front door shuts and you brace yourself for a lecture. Instead, Eustace walks in with a stout woman.

"Hi there," she says and actually shakes your hand. "I'm Rosabelle."

"Super. Regale us with something fascinating about yourself, Rosabelle."

Eustace glares at you.

Rosabelle smiles. "I'm originally from Arkansas. Moved out here three years ago since there's a good job market for my profession."

"Because of all the fatsos?"

"I'm trained to help the morbidly obese live a more comfortable lifestyle."

"Of course," you say. "And what if that person is not morbidly obese but happily so?"

"Could be. But I haven't found that to be true yet with my bed-bound clients."

You instantly hate her face.

"And what sorts of clients have you cared for in the past?" Eustace asks.

"Truthfully, older women," she says. "But what matters most to me is making real connections. No matter who you are, emotional support can help you achieve a physical goal."

"That's lovely," Eustace says.

"No, it's not. I'm a man."

"What about you?" Rosabelle asks. "What's your story?"

MOUTH

"Car accident," you say. Eustace is spinning away in Rosabelle's allure. You can't lose her. "I got T-boned by my wife on her way home from work one night."

Eustace drops her head into her hands. You've never said it out loud before, but it's the truth. You'd had a few with Ren and Davey at the bar. Mostly light beers, though, so you were fine to drive. Buzzed at worst, nothing unsafe. It was almost midnight in June, the road slick with oil and the lingering puddles of a thunderstorm, but you'd gunned it to make the light. Eustace happened to be the first car in the turn lane, hurrying home after a long shift at work. Your yellow had turned red as you barreled through the intersection; Eustace was just as quick on her green.

"An accident." Eustace dabs her eyes with a sleeve.

Rosabelle nods.

"Well, you've made my wife cry, so we're done here." You extend your hand, feeling dirty that you sold out your wife. But at least it worked. Besides, nothing happened to Eustace after the accident—it's not like she got fat. You can apologize to her later. "Thank you for your time today. Eustace will show you out."

Rosabelle stands, but studies you. "No matter who you select as your caretaker, I hope you get assistance with your self-sabotage."

"You're hired," Eustace says.

You flap your arms. "What? No! I don't like her."

"Everything she said is true," Eustace says. "I can't be your nurse forever. I need to have my own life again. Maybe I'm making it worse for you."

"But I need you here, Eustace."

Eustace shakes her head. "Rosabelle, can you start Friday at eight?"

"I think that could be worked out."

A steaming beef burrito floats across the television screen, all cheddar cheese and sour cream, only two dollars. Defeated, you shut your eyes, pointing and flexing until the commercial is over, wishing you could fit in the jeep.

***

Once Rosabelle took a grand tour of the house, helped you onto your scooter, and got back in her car, Eustace iced you out, saying she was going on a walk. Something about needing to "clear the energy." Well, she's not the only one.

"I've been invisible long enough," you fume to Steve as you motor to the doorway. Eustace thinks she can just desert you after all she's put you through, but you're not that weak. Now, staring down the thirty-foot walkway, you're ready to take control. You heave your body off the wheelchair. You will get the mail.

Instead of your usual slippers, you managed to slide on your Velcro slip-ons with the help of Granddad's old tortoiseshell shoehorn. Each shoe is fifteen inches long, so if you put one in front of the other and employ positive visualization, you'll only have to move your feet twenty-one times to get to the mailbox.

After lodging a rolled up *Outdoor Life* magazine between the screen door and the lock, you step down onto the cracked concrete, shuffling off your first step. Move. Stop. Move. Tremble. Stop. You're absolutely soaked, but here you are, eight steps out of the house on your own. Wheeze, your thighs burning like you just hustled up the mudbank. Left foot, right, kneecaps quaking, your muscles slowly recalling the motion of walking.

"Enjoying the sun today?" your neighbor, Stan, hollers from his driveway as he soaps his Deville. A man in his late seventies, pumping his toothpick arms every morning during his pre-breakfast walk in light blue tear-away pants and a sleeveless Alice Cooper T-shirt.

You waggle your fingers in a sort of wave. By the time you touch the sun-warmed mailbox, sweat has waterfalled over the collar of your T-shirt, past your pits, soaking your waistband.

"You good?"

As you open your mouth to respond, the oak trees spin to the left.

***

Squinting into the wide sky, you wonder if this is the great blue expanse you've heard about. You search for Grammy Louise or your cousin Rutherford who died of meningitis in the seventh grade.

"It's just a tumble. Everything's going to be a-okay." A liver-spotted hand blocks the sun and your view. "Can I help you up?"

You push against the gravel until you're upright, albeit winded. There's asphalt. Signs for Piccolo Court and Tenth Avenue—your street. People staring. Stan and a few neighbors come closer, their faces scrunched with worry, eyes like spotlights. Everyone is focused on you.

"We can call for help, sir," the widow from across the street says.

You sniff for gasoline first and then listen for an ambulance. Have you been hit again or did you just fall? Hopefully you've been hit so you'd have an excuse to be splayed in the street. Flexing what's left of your weakened calf muscles, you check for sensation.

"Come on, now," Stan says. "Got to try."

"Am I okay? Tell me where I'm bleeding!" Prodding your chin and forehead, you study each finger for signs of wounds.

"No blood," he says. "You just need to get up."

"It'll take me some time."

"Eddie, can you call for an ambulance?"

The question socks you into clarity. You imagine Eustace's beautiful face, her eyes elongated funhouse mirrors when she finds her fat pathetic husband beached in a gutter, so big that a Volkswagen has to swerve into a different lane just to drive around him. You imagine how you'd look on television right now—like a monstrous dollop of sweatpants and shame, you sad babyman. A wail sounds from your mouth, detonating so deep it even surprises you. Someone rubs your back slowly, light circles, warm, reassuring. The attention makes you feel like a real person now. Completely loved, you let the tears fall.

"It's okay, sugar."

"I'm so embarrassed," you say.

"Don't be, you're with good people. Are you in pain?"

"Yes."

They coo over you, these kind people who rushed to your aid without any judgment, neighbors you've never even waved to before. Piled on the curb with gravel clinging to your palms, you relax into their love, all muddy and sweaty, just as Eustace dashes across the driveway.

"What happened, honey? Are you okay?"

Such relief. You bawl, and as your face flushes and the hiccups sputter out, her strong arms wrap around you, protecting you. For the moment, it's just you and her cocooned together, as it should be.

***

Once they stuff you onto your scooter and guide you back inside the house, all the humiliation, rage, and vulnerability has emptied you out, cutting down to the raw edges of your hunger.

"Do we have any cookies?" you ask.

"C'mon, now's not the time."

"But I want some, Eustace."

"Stop it. You don't need them."

"Get them for me! I've been through enough." As you rattle the table, you overturn cooking magazines, knocking bariatric pamphlets and hospital forms to the floor.

Sighing, Eustace yanks down the pink and white frosted circus cookies she keeps stashed for herself in the top cupboard.

Each bite feels like a long hug.

***

THURSDAY, JUNE 19

"Thanks anyway, Rosabelle," you say and then hang up.

The Thursday morning light halves you, your shoulders cool in the darkness of dawn, but your legs casting a fluorescent white glow as light sears through the living room window. Dust twirls, rising from the carpet, the curtains, and your body, stale flakes that you've already inhaled and processed countless times today, every day for the past two years. After your big fall, you were able to persuade Eustace to roll your bed closer to the entryway, giving you a different outlook on the room. She'd even added two pillows. From your new dent in the mattress, the calendar is in view, a thick black X through today's date. A new date yet to be circled.

"Eustace!" you call from your pillows.

"What?" she asks, leaning in from the kitchen, her hair frizzy from the steam and heat of washing dishes.

"My leg. I can't move it."

"Did you try?"

"Yes," you lie. "But I need help."

She sighs. "Just give me five minutes to finish these pans."

You hear her banging the roasting pan in the sink while she scrubs, water splashing onto the floor and countertops, which she'll also have to wipe down. Your leg feels like it's getting singed.

"Eustace, my leg is burning."

She hurls the pan into the sink and, hands soaked, comes over, grabbing behind your knee to adjust your leg. Soapy water spills down your thigh.

"There," she huffs. "You happy?"

The sheets, damp with dishwater, feel cool against the sweaty width of your legs. Heaped atop the pillows, your wife within eyesight, you stare at Steve. Under his wide, watchful eye, you smile and take a long sip from your Coke.

YOU AND YOUR COLD SOVIET HEART

As soon as Jupiter Valentine shuffles outside to check the snowfall, October cracks him across the face. Seven in the morning and daybreak is just a pinhole in the darkness, the yard hushed blue with moonlit snow. He shoves his fingers into a pile on the windowsill. It's dumped a good two-knuckles' worth overnight. His walkway is frozen slick, the birch trees gilded white. Winter taunts early in Fairbanks.

Jupiter swallows the last of his coffee. On days like this, when simply flipping open the comforter feels like a bushwhack, his buddies at the worksite go on about how their wives brew them fresh coffee every morning, maybe even fry up some fatback. He sucks coffee grounds from his teeth, his stomach rumbling. An iced wind knifes through his robe and as he shivers, he cranes his neck checking if the auroras are out. When he was small, Jupiter thought he'd be able to hear those long green ribbons snapping across the sky, something metallic, like chains knocking in the wind. But once he realized that they simply shift, a silent burn and fade, he began staring hard into the sky, hoping to will them there instead. Jupiter squints up at the fading night. Nothing.

There are plenty of boxes stacked tall on the porch, though, each one with the same return address: *Ruby Owens, Issaquah, WA*. After six months of plane fares and teary airport goodbyes,

Ruby was moving to be with him, and it felt like finding the perfect work boot.

 He drags the load inside. She'd made him promise not to open anything so they could set up the house together, hang all her dresses next to his snow bibs. Fine with him, though it's unreal how much crap she's sent. Eighteen boxes so far. When would it stop? To fend off his stress, he dials her number.

 "Hello, baby," Ruby answers. "How are you?"

 "On top of the world," he says, his automatic response to anyone in the lower forty-eight. A jet engine roars in the background. "You working?"

 "Sorry, Jupiter, got a departure. Call you later? Delta 1553!" She blows a kiss into the receiver, hanging up before he can respond.

 Ruby works as an air-traffic controller at Sea-Tac airport, a job she'd coveted as a child tracking crop dusters that skimmed the Yakima Valley. Speeding away from the family dairy business after college, she barreled straight toward the FAA Academy in Oklahoma City. And now, a big shot controlling Departures in Seattle, she sneaks gushy phone calls to him between her two-hour shifts.

 "Hi, sweetie. Can't wait to be in your arms again. Only a few more months." Then with the same breath, she'll yell, "Ascend! Climb to five thousand!"

 Ruby's hair has a sheen that sends hunters out for black bears in the fall. Definitely the hottest chick he's ever been with. And fancy, too. She even bought herself a pair of real diamond studs for her thirty-eighth birthday. Most of the women bellying up at his bars in Fairbanks wear jade or silver.

And now he's about to settle down. After all the different ladies from the Howling Dog Saloon, the lust that inevitably petered out after three months, his own parents' divorces, he never thought he'd marry. Nothing sad about it, just something to accept, like crooked teeth. But he was getting older and his buddies had already taken the plunge.

"You planning on living the bachelor life forever, Valentine?" Reggie, one of the guys from the worksite, would ask far too often.

"If I'm lucky. Why? You jealous I can do whatever I want?"

"No coochie in the world will keep me from caribou season. But wifeing up has its perks. You just have to lay down your rules early so she knows you're not playing. Otherwise it all goes south and she'll get ya," he said, tapping his temple.

That blew his mind. Ruby was the one who decided she'd move to Alaska. Just dropped it into their conversation one night while she was putting together a veggie burger for dinner.

"Jupiter, it's where you are, and I want to be with you. Besides," she added, "I know you'll never leave."

Leave? Where else could he possibly live? It takes a certain steed to survive in Fairbanks; Alaska marrows through his bones. And in three weeks, Ruby will be making French toast in his kitchen, leaving long hairs plastered to his shower walls, sticking her ice-cold feet on his at bedtime every day for the rest of his life.

"Issaquah's a forest," she'd said. "I'll just be moving from one forest to another."

***

Jupiter starts every morning with black coffee and two poached eggs, so while the water boils, he sits at his computer, tapping out Dio riffs until his homepage appears on the screen. Behind him, the water heater knocks like it won't hold through the new year. He scrolls through his three favorite sites: KTUU News, the latest NHL scores, any hot additions to *Olga Love!*

Irina: Blonde, smoker, no children. St. Petersburg.

Self-Description: *I'm funny but can be so serious if it is needed. I'm nice and loving. My favorite holiday is New Year. I like to stay at home near to the favorite person, communicating with him or even simply to keep silent.*

Comments: *I want him loving, gentle, and thoughtful. He must love me and our children, if we will have them.*

She was all overbite, her mouth having forgotten the movement of laughter.

Ekaterina: Brunette, attended University, no children. Moscow.

Self-Description: *I work as engineer at the building company. I live alone but I would like to have family with many children. If you have children, it is nice, but I would like to have our own children. By my character, I'm cheerful and honest. I enjoy reading, meeting with friend, computer, going in the theatres.*

Comments: *I hope to have in the future a happy family with a serious man. You will be kind and I reckon honest about real* *meeting, real relationships. I am wanting one man who is happy and willing to start family with children.*

Ekaterina advertises with a side shot, which means she's cross-eyed. And at least eight years older than the thirty-six she claims. Behind him, the water bubbles.

"Have you ever wanted kids?" Ruby once asked.

"Never." He hadn't meant to spit it out like rancid elk. But, at thirty-nine, Ruby wasn't young, and at forty-two, neither was he; there was age in the ways they patterned their lives. Jupiter tried to imagine himself backcountry skiing with a toddler or getting one to stop screaming in Fred Meyer. He'd never even held a baby.

At the time, he'd grabbed a red plastic rose from the vase between them, presenting it to her to stifle the silence that was stretching too long.

Ruby had giggled. "Even the damn flowers are frozen here."

"You'll see," he said. "Everything thaws eventually."

Tatiana: Brunette, some drinking. Minsk.

Self-Description: *I am open, friendly, with good humors. I have many hobbies. I love movies, cars, body shaping. I enjoy being in the nature and like friendly company. I dream to meet a pleasant man and live happily. My strong point is my character. I dislike lie. My favorite quotation: "Everything is done for good."*

Comments: *I am looking for a attractive big-arm brunette man of 40–55 years, reliable and honest. I think that mutual understanding is the basis of ideal relationship. No childrens, simply us.*

He studies Tatiana's lips, those hypnotic green eyes, like she's spread eagle on the bed waiting for him. Still there, after all this time.

***

Nine months ago, Jupiter had flown to Seattle for the annual Union Fifty-Seven celebration, thinking only of Chivas and Cohibas with the railroad boys. Then a curvy thing in a tight gray pantsuit strut into the conference room. Jupiter had tripped over something—his boot, his jaw—and all his buddies roared, their laughter trailing him like an untucked shirt as he hurried into the aviation section to sit behind her. His eyes bored into the back of her head, the indents of her waist, enjoying how she rubbed away the tension between her shoulder blades. Ruby was classy in red lipstick and pointy black heels, impracticalities for the ladies he knew. After a few rounds of intense eye contact, she spun around and whispered, "Either introduce yourself or keep staring and I clock you. Your choice." They spent the rest of the weekend in her hotel room, sweaty and acrobatic.

"We should do something wild," Ruby had said on her last night, both of them buck naked.

"I'm into it." He'd been desperate to try anal. "How crazy do you want to get?"

"You should marry me."

Jupiter bellowed. "Too crazy."

"This weekend has been amazing. Don't you want to keep it going?"

"Sure. But marriage sounds a little nuts."

"Oh yeah? And what exactly do you have to lose up in Old Snowtown?" she asked, crawling across the floor.

"My freedom. My privacy. Half my cash."

Ruby dangled her breasts above his mouth. "You're all alone up there. Don't you want someone to keep you warm?"

"You think you could handle it?"

"For you, yes." She lowered herself to his lips. "It could be like this every day."

He licked her nipple. "You promise?"

"I do."

Just like that.

Jupiter lifts the boxes and tests their weight, hoping her scent will drift out from the packing tape. The thought of Ruby wearing one of those lacy red numbers excites him until he's snow blind, unhinging his utility knife. As he slits open the first box, a stack of sweaters puffs out, smelling of Ruby's neck. Another box bursts with cookbooks, wrinkled slow cooker recipes. His face burns.

Fluffy robes, jeans, hair products. Ripping through the cardboard, he peers at the things Ruby wants in her new northern home. His home—1,569 square feet of carpet he vacuums when he feels like it, a shower he scrubs maybe every other month, trash he doesn't always toss back in the can when it bounces off the lip. And now, all this.

Then he notices it, tucked inside the last box like a dirty sock. Sky blue and tiny, with "Daddy's Little Star" embroidered on a baseball between the sleeves.

Jupiter stretches the shirt over his hand, his fingertips jutting through the neck. It's soft, sewn for little limbs and drool. Softer than anything he's ever owned, even his most ancient fleece. The price tag is attached: $19.99. He'd spent that much on a pound of good halibut two weeks ago.

Jupiter tears it off. It lands on some old popcorn kernels he thought he'd whisked under the stove.

***

He hustles through the garage gripping his work vest and hard hat, the wind chill slapping with the iced palm of dawn. He hasn't been with her in two months. Ripping the plug from the antifreeze outlet, he lets the engine warm while he picks at a scab on his finger. She swore she was on the pill, so how could it possibly be his? There are miles and mountains between them; he'd never know if she'd been creeping around. Until now.

Jupiter backs out and speeds down the street, his truck sliding on the road ice. Has she been lying to his face this whole time? He'd be funding that kid until he was sixty, thousands of his sweat-soaked dollars wasted on LEGOs and braces and Little League equipment. No wonder she's so anxious to get to Alaska, now that she's finished banging her way through Seattle metropolitan. Jupiter can just picture it. Rodney, that goateed douche who controls the radar. Rodney ripping the gold buttons off her blouse as he rams her against the pop machine, grunting like a musk ox, making her call him "Rod." Or even worse, Paul, the mouth-breather in Ground Control. Jupiter gasses the truck, imagining their pasty bodies ghost-like and rocking in the darkened tower. Ruby moaning. Paul. Paul. He slams the brakes.

A moose and calf block the road, staring into his headlights. Jupiter smacks the dashboard and honks. Angling her broad body, the moose turns toward him with her head lowered. Jupiter presses on the clutch and downshifts while she edges closer, ears flattened, primed to charge.

"Come on," Jupiter hisses, glancing around. "I don't have time for this shit."

The road is hemmed with spruce trees, the air clear and biting. It's a ten-minute drive to the nearest house—too far to walk in this weather, especially if he's hurt. Jupiter revs the engine. The calf ambles toward some leaves on a low branch, but the moose steps closer toward the truck, one knobby leg kicking forward. She misses his headlight and blinks, rolling the whites of her eyes.

"Fuck it."

Jupiter guns the truck around them but it fishtails, bed swaying, the terrible screech of twisting metal. He lurches with the animal's impact, the seat belt straining against his chest until a snowdrift buffets the truck and straightens him out.

In the rearview mirror, he watches the calf slump to the ground. The moose looms over it, lips pulled back, moaning low and long. Jupiter cranks the radio and keeps on driving.

***

Once he makes it to the tented construction site, Jupiter stumbles across the ice, beelining to the portable office for coffee.

"Morning, bud," Reggie says. "Frozen yet?"

"Down to my balls."

"Seriously. Can't wait until this shit melts."

Morning trickles through the worksite like a watercolor, wet and wan, just after nine. Jupiter sweats, the jackhammer strong in his grip, the air hazy with sunlight and snow dust, as Al, their foreman, strides by.

"You think that's going all the way through, Valentine?"

Jupiter stands to survey his work.

"Gotta beat the frost, man." Jupiter hammers harder, the earth shattering into a cold fissur around him.

***

After microwaving a frozen meatloaf dinner, Jupiter keeps his fingers busy by checking the snow report. He shakes out his comforter, sorts the recycling, organizes fish marinades in the fridge. Then his fingers dial Ruby's number.

"Hey baby," she says. "United clear for takeoff. I can't believe I'm moving to Fairbanks. Never would've thought I'd end up there."

"We should talk, Ruby."

"Hold short, runway three-four. What's that, Jupiter?"

He coughs, hoping to clear the choke from his throat. "I'm not doing this."

"I can't read those coordinates. Jupiter, I'll call you tonight. Love you. Climb and maintain, Alpha." She hangs up.

Grabbing the tape gun, he starts sealing boxes with thick strips of duct tape.

***

MOUTH

Jupiter scrolls through Tatiana's profile again two hours later. He'd emailed her once a year ago, right before he met Ruby. That was back when he couldn't stand to hear the woman he'd been sleeping with, a woman who could field-dress a deer in less than twenty minutes, bitching and moaning about not getting her ex's military benefits. Jupiter wanted something easy. No drama. Tatiana had replied with a letter and a Western Union form, but he'd met Ruby that weekend so he never responded.

Tatiana gazes at him.

***

Ruby calls after she gets home and pours a glass of merlot. "Some days, these damn planes come in all at once."

Jupiter's tongue lists, dry in his mouth. "Sorry."

"But I'm in bed now. In bed with my man."

He clears his throat.

"So, Alaska," she says. "Just three more weeks! I can't wait. Tell me the story again?"

His nerves bend and crack, so he clenches his fists to steady his hands. "Alaska is twice as big as Texas. Seventeen of the twenty highest mountain peaks in North America can be found here."

"And Russia! Do the thing."

Jupiter digs deep for his most exaggerated movie accent. One last time. "Da, neighbor. Ve vill valk over and invade your cahntry."

Her laughter twinkles through the ice-cracked night, bouncing into his house and off her boxes now labeled with his return address. "Do you think I can pet a moose?"

"Ruby."

"Wait, before you say anything else, I have a surprise for you."

"No—"

"I'm naked."

Jupiter forces himself to think of mangled Dall sheep. The pipeline explosion. Great-grandma Jane's milk burps.

"I'm naked for you, Jupiter."

Impalement.

"What do you want to do now?" Her breath quickens.

Helicopter crashes. Bankruptcy.

"I'll do anything," she taunts.

Chernobyl. Leprosy. A baby. "I want you to stop."

"What? Why?"

"I saw it." He focuses on his bouncing knee. "I went through all your crap."

Her silence numbs the line.

"I told you I didn't want kids, and now you're suddenly pregnant?" Jupiter stands. "Pretty clever way to lock me down. I'll just pay for everything from here on out, right?"

"I wanted to look you in the eye when I told you. It's not something you share over the phone: 'Guess what? We're going to be parents.' I must've missed some pills. I've been so stressed out with the move, and work, and this wedding we need to plan. The baby was an accident."

He paces, slipping on his ratty throw rugs. "I don't want a damn kid, especially one that's not even mine."

"What's the matter with you? Of course it's yours, Jupiter."

"Is that what your friends told you to say?"

She bawls. "This doesn't make any sense."

He knows he's doing damage, the deep rotting kind that crept into grandpa's old Chena Hot Springs cabin, the smell of insulation reeking as mold bloomed with the spring thaw. And like the mold, he can't stop. "This is not how I want my life to be. I want it to go back to the way it was."

"But you can't. It's too late now."

"Not if you get rid of it." A chill walks into the room and drags its nails over his skin.

"Are you crazy?" she asks. "I'm thirty-nine."

"Exactly."

She says nothing for so long, he wonders if she hung up. "So?" he asks.

"I told my friends you were different. But they were right." She's stopped crying, her voice stabbing like morning icicles. "You really would rather just stay up there freezing cold, in your shithole house, rationing out your love."

Jupiter slumps, staring at the boxes. The water heater ticks and strains. "I'm sending all your stuff back this weekend."

"You're running away because this got too real."

"No," he says. "I'm staying right here."

"And that's what's sad," she says before the dial tone fills his ears.

***

The next day, the boys crunch through the dirty parking lot snow toward the tented worksite while Jupiter storms ahead.

"What's your deal, Valentine? Morning wood getting to you?"

"Ruby's pregnant."

"No shit? Hey, congrats!"

"I'm not the right guy."

"It's not yours?"

"Doubt it."

"Wow. Sorry, man."

"Doesn't matter. Don't want it."

Inside the tent, Reggie pulls him aside. "When all's said and done, if the kid's not yours, you're off the hook. In the meantime, what you need is someone with better sense, someone who lets you drive." He pulls a napkin from his pocket and scribbles on it. "Check out these dolls."

Jupiter glances down, his face betraying him.

"Don't freak, they're not hookers. Just good girls looking for international relationships. You pick the one you want, from hair color to language. Easiest way to find your dream girl." Reggie grins. "How do you think I met Karina?"

Karina, quiet and busty, was right at home in the Fairbanks extremes. They'd been married for six years and had a baby girl. "Straight out of Belarus for only five thousand bucks. Same price as a good used camper." Reggie winks. "Trust me. *Olga Love!*"

"Good to know," Jupiter says, shoving the napkin in his back pocket.

***

Later that night, Jupiter puts in seven hours at the computer, skipping dinner. The women unfold on the screen. Oksana, Marina, Anastasia, bedraggled with stony eyes and thin lips, backgrounds of thievery or tanneries he bet. He scrolled past them. He wasn't anyone's meal ticket. The others are pretty enough, like day-old pastries. He should've taken this route in the first place and kept it easy: his turf, his life, a good-looking woman. No compromises.

Jupiter clicks back to his favorite profile. Tatiana. Her name unfurls from the tongue, a white flag waving him in. She's attended vocational school, works as a cashier. Probably not too mouthy. Once again, he adds her to his "Hot List" and waits for the agency to email him.

***

December furies across Fairbanks, the road snow dingy with pine needles, salt, used antifreeze. Holiday lights glint across the neighborhood. Feeling festive, Jupiter had nailed a strand around the front of his house for Tatiana's first Christmas with him. And now, with Ruby's boxes gone, there's enough room in his house for a tree. He'd even stuck a star on top.

Digging sleep from his eyes, Jupiter shuffles through his mail. Cable bill, pizza ad, coupon for the shooting range, letter from Minsk, card from Issaquah. His stomach drops. Ruby had called a few times, leaving him raging messages detailing what a bastard he was. What could he say to that?

He slices open the letter from Minsk. A form for Western Union falls out, along with a wallet photo of a brunette. Jupiter smells it.

Dear Jupiter,

I would like to meet you. Would you like to meet me? If yes, please send 15,000RUB so I pay bus ticket to Moscow airport. I promise you like me.

All my love,
Tatiana
PS: I read Jupiter is biggest planet. Handsome!

She sounds just like her bio. No way someone could fake a flirtation like that. Jupiter studies her face, a triangular chin that would fit perfectly in his hand. Even with black stenciled eyebrows, she's hot, like she knows he wants to be spanked. He stirs. Backlit with violet lighting, she cradles a pink rose against her cheek, her pale skin free from acne or scars. He makes a note to refinance the house.

Then he grabs the envelope from Issaquah. He's refused contact with Ruby since their break-up, a freeze-out technique mastered in tenth grade and used successfully ever since. Tearing it open, he finds a yellow card with a balloon that reads "Celebration!" He shakes it, hoping for a check to cover the cost of shipping her stuff back. Instead, there's a photo taped to the left side with *Yours!!!* written under it.

Sinking into his recliner, he squints at the picture. It's blurry, gray and black. Big see-through head, white lima bean center. Not like a baby at all. Closer to an alien and he doesn't believe in those. He tosses the photo in the trash can and returns to the computer.

***

Jupiter's fingers tremble as he dials the long row of numbers.

"Allo. Dobroe utro."

"Hi. Hello? Tatiana?"

"Allo? Yes?"

"It's Jupiter Valentine? For our three o'clock phone call."

She squeals. "Husband!"

"Not yet." He smiles. "How do I know it's you, Tatiana?"

"Because we have same soul. I fly to Alaskia to love you."

He studies her photo, trying to match the voice with the face. "Yes, you fly here. To me."

Then Tatiana sounds sad, her voice dropping to a whimper. "But money. I have none."

Jupiter pictures her pouting, those shiny lips collapsing like snow-laden branches. Worse, he imagines the slow flow of tears down her perfect cheeks. "I will send you money. For visa. And ticket. I'll send the papers."

Another squeal. "Send rubles a Western Union? I come ten days!"

"Next week?"

"Too much?"

"No. It's perfect, Tatiana."

"Be seen soon! Send rubles. Do svidaniya! Chao!"

Plenty of girls will say anything just to get into the States—he's recorded the exposés on *Dateline*. But Tatiana's been on the site way too long to be pretending she wants a husband. And she sounds just like that sexy corporal in the James Bond movie. She's real. After authorizing an advance on his debit card for the plane ticket, he spends the rest of the evening filling out Western Union forms.

***

Jupiter smoothes gel into his hair, tugging upward so the balding patch in back is less noticeable. Then he sprays his neck—and boxers—with the Brut cologne he'd bought for the occasion. Judging by her online profile, she should be a foot shorter than him. Thinner than Ruby. And hopefully with bigger boobs. He squeezes the plush moose he's brought instead of flowers. Of all people, Tatiana will understand it's too cold to grow roses on top of the world.

A cloudy morning elbows out the fading night sky as he speeds to the airport. No auroras. But the frozen Chena River glitters, an ice shelf of diamonds. And he's called in sick to work, first time in eight years. He can't believe it.

Fairbanks International buzzes. Dodging the incoming crab fishermen, all salty and wave-worn, Jupiter hurries to the waiting area and stands casually in front, as if he's not two hours early. As if he's calm. Just like he practiced. He clutches his sign: *Tatiana.*

An hour passes. He scurries to the bathroom once, sprinting back to the monitors to make sure he hasn't missed her flight. Passengers and employees crowd past him, his heart slamming while his eyes scan. Snowboards, luggage. Jupiter's palms sweat on the plush moose until he's embarrassed by its dampness. He billows his shirt.

The desk agent calls him over. "Do you need something, sir?"

Jupiter points to his sign. "Is there a woman named Tatiana on the next flight?"

"Are you a family member?"

"Not yet."

"I'm sorry," the desk agent says. "But unless you're related or married, I can't print any passenger manifests."

Sitting on the edge of a chair under the fluorescent buzz, Jupiter rubs the back of his neck. It's been four hours. Maybe Moscow is snowed in. CNN says it's sleeting in Tokyo. He has one mint left, so he slips it into his pocket for their first kiss.

After two hours, the agent shuts off the lights at the desk. "Sir, no other flights are due in tonight. Merry Christmas," she says, hurrying past him.

Outside, the snow has cut in sideways as if someone tipped the snowglobe. Steeling to the wind, Jupiter walks to his truck. In the darkness above, a plane departs, two red beams pushing into the night. As they merge, a slow whip of green flares across the sky. Jupiter chucks the moose in the snow.

He could call Reggie, though Reggie will be busy, tied up in fatherly commitments. Instead, Jupiter will head home to the liquor stashed above the fridge, his tracks disappearing in the snow, a man assured by a compass that points only to himself, dwarfed by his own false north, the green whisper twisting tighter.

BIRDS OF PARADISE

Oranges from the neighbor's tree hung heavy and low, pushing over the fence and into Camille's yard. Something rustled the dry palm fronds beneath the utility pole. Ninety-three degrees and a Stage One smog alert: summer in LA, a sepiascape teeming with lizards and pill bugs, the endless surge and pop of paleolithic tar. As she hid in the citrus-laced shade, Camille surveyed her progress. There was still so much to do.

Shuffling into the sun along her suburban strip of lawn, she carried a trash lid loaded with dandelions and bent down, wincing when the pain seared her stomach again. It'd been months of this, fifty unwanted pounds and a burn like knife-hits deep in the hollows of her belly. So she waited it out by counting red fire ants as they dashed across the concrete. Once the dizziness subsided, she knelt, as slow as a grandmother, ensuring her new acrylics didn't scrape on the scalded concrete, and ripped out a tattered agapanthus. That left her birds of paradise to firework green, tangerine, indigo, all straining angles against the patio. Their leaves had crisped into a yellow translucence, but the buds were firm and vibrant, each one gawking left, exasperated with the summer scorch.

"That thing's dead," Gage said, his chest sausage pink. "Maybe you should let it go already."

"It's not dead—check out the buds. I'm bringing it back."

"Or we could get you another plant."

"No, I want this one. I've been working on it forever."

"Look who's too cool."

"The coolest girl you know."

Once he turned back toward the sun, she snipped off a bud and tucked it inside her pocket.

"Ready for the doc tomorrow?" he asked, chugging his Slurpee.

"Nope." As Camille tipped a plastic watering can to the baked dirt, the water rolled away in quick rivulets. She ran her tongue over her lips. July left everything dry-mouthed.

"You sure you don't want me to go with you? I could be that handsome guy in the waiting room, cringing between toddlers."

Camille smiled. "Don't flatter yourself."

Best friends since tenth grade, Gage and Camille had solaced each other through their suburban rage with mixed tapes of Sonic Youth and Liz Phair. At their most rebellious, they'd chugged wine coolers in the park, maybe raided his Aunt Marina's weed stash. But they always made it to first period and eventually CalState Long Beach. Now, twenty years later, both were still single, still renters. A bitterness that flared during bouquet tosses.

They'd had one drunken moment two years ago, pressing close together while the moonlit waves lifted and sparkled under the Manhattan Beach Pier ("Haven't you ever wondered what could happen?" "But you're like a sister."), eventually stumbling onto a friend's futon later that evening. Hammered, they'd forgotten a condom and she'd let it go, trusting he was clean. Things were strained for a few weeks, but nothing a bumbling talk over margaritas couldn't fix. She'd been nervous until he'd grinned and swept her into a big bear hug outside Mijares restaurant saying, "We got that out of our systems." Although they'd remained close, escorting each other through the hilarities and humiliations of career successes and social failures, she'd never forgotten how safe it'd felt to sleep with his arm curling around her. After all those years, when she'd tried so hard to come off unaffected, to bite back her jealousy every time she met one of his stupid new girlfriends, she had shown him what he really meant to her. And she was surprised by how she ached for him, still.

***

"Undress from the waist down. Gown opens in the front," the nurse said. "Dr. Langley will be with you shortly." She shut the door behind her.

As a child, Camille couldn't wait for her nine o'clock bedtime, the moment her parents closed the door after tucking her in. That click meant freedom, the chance to cartwheel through history books, romances, and legends, past the plastic confines of California all the way to Stonehenge or Easter Island or the gold rush. Now, in a room where the sole reading material was how to do a breast self-exam, Camille had to improvise. She stripped off her jeans and furtively hid her underwear inside them, folding the set with a precision known only to Navy SEALs and women at the gyno. Then she wrapped the paper gown around as much of herself as it'd cover, easing into calming reveries of castles and courtly love.

"Knock, knock," Dr. Langley said as he entered.

She shook Lancelot from her thoughts and crossed her legs protectively. "Hello."

"Nice to see you again." He perched on the stool facing her.

Camille sat close enough to smell the lunchtime curry clinging to his overcoat. Wait, did he remember her vagina? She tightened her legs. A male gynecologist! Men, forever trying to get into a woman's pants. And the audacity of one thinking he could be an expert on it. The only reason she saw Dr. Langley was because she didn't have to take the freeway to his office. She rubbed her arms, the gown crinkling like a hamburger wrapper.

"How old are you now?"

"Thirty-six."

"Do you drink?"

She considered her debilitating hangover from the weekend, another eighty-degree day slumped on the couch inhaling pizza rolls and *True Hollywood Story* until her Pad See Ew arrived. If only In-N-Out delivered. "Yeah, a few times a week."

"Are you a smoker?"

She could sense an evangelical background behind his gold-rimmed glasses as he studied her for tattoos, one too many silver studs dotting her ears.

"I might have a cigarette when I drink," she said. Or a nice tight joint on a Saturday when she needed to relax.

"And what types of pain have you been experiencing?"

"My period has been off. I get intense cramps, can't keep breakfast down. Random dizziness. Plus, I put on fifty pounds."

"Any chance you could be pregnant?"

She snickered. "I haven't been with anyone in two years. So if I'm knocked up, we'll need to place an emergency call to *That's Incredible!*"

"I'm sorry?"

Oh boy, her anxiety was gunning for it now, straight to inappropriate laughter. What treachery, this instinct that crested at funerals and love scenes in Colin Firth movies. Her face burned. "It's a show from the eighties? Fran Tarkenton was one of the hosts."

He shook his head and patted the wax-papered exam table. "Scoot to the edge and relax."

The stirrups, the cold metal instruments, the fact that he sported a headlamp during the exam. She grimaced. Who could possibly relax knowing their most delicate parts were about to get invaded by salad tongs and a scrape? Camille kept her Sketchers on so she'd feel less vulnerable spread open before someone's face, a sensation she'd enjoy any other time.

"Are you interested in having children?"

She held her breath as he inserted the speculum. "Not sure. I haven't really thought about it."

"Well, you're thirty-six."

An entire adulthood spent trying to dodge date rape, herpes, married men. How many hours of her life had she spent consoling her friends through those crises? Most of them had eventually found love and paired off, tucking away their ugly memories like wings that had forgotten how to fly. Camille had been so careful, except for that one time with Gabe, and considered herself lucky to come out unscathed. "Guess I just haven't met the right guy."

A magazine photo of Tom Cruise had been taped to the ceiling, all squinty and cocksure. Nothing like a mini alpha with an alien overlord complex to really calm a woman! Instead, Camille envisioned her old go-to: Val Kilmer, all greased-up, flexing in the volleyball scene from *Top Gun*. Dr. Langley slid out the speculum and just as she was about to exhale into the tanned glory of Iceman stretching up and over the net, the doctor went back in with two gloved fingers. A *Cosmo* article once said not wrinkling the forehead would help an anxious woman relax down there, so she shut her eyes to the gelled strands draping Tom's smug grin and unclenched her teeth. Iceman. The room smelled of bandages and lubricant.

"Right there," Dr. Langley said, pushing harder on the left side of her abdomen as his fingers probed. "That's concerning."

***

Camille had parked at the edge of the lot near a low concrete wall. Panicking from the driver's seat, she stared at the cracked asphalt of Colorado Boulevard, its tarry veins scarred by the weight of petal-heavy Rose Parade floats and weekend cruisers. Beige exhaust shrouded the valley basin, while million-dollar homes glitzed the mountainside, higher and higher, ruthless grabs for any kind of downtown view. As heat waves shimmered around her, she flipped through the pamphlets the nurse had stacked in her hand before she left—uterine cancer, cysts, reproductive disorders—and called Gage.

"Hey," he whispered into the phone. "I'm at lunch with Hot Girl from the tenth floor. Third time this week!"

Camille recoiled like someone had licked her cheek. Three times and he hadn't mentioned her until now? "That's great."

"She's also seen all five original *Planet of the Apes* movies."

"And which one's her favorite?"

"The first one, obviously, before the make-up got bad."

Her laugh sounded like a tennis ball bouncing across an empty court. She sat taller, hoping she hadn't rattled the mass.

"Tomorrow I'm taking her to that belly-dancing joint you love in Glendale," he said. "Anyway, how'd the appointment go?"

"It was all right."

"Did the doc stick you on a no-booze, no-carb diet? If so, let me know so I can find a new best friend."

"No, it's just some lady problems."

"Like what?"

"Are you going to give me another exam right now?"

"Cut the shit, Camille. What'd he say?"

She cracked a window. "He felt a mass in there and wants to get it checked out. I'm going for a CT scan tomorrow."

"Does he think it's cancer or something?"

"Gage, do we really need to talk about tumors during your date? I'll be fine. It's probably just fibroids. Go have fun, I'll talk to you later."

"I don't like this."

"She's waiting for you."

"Promise you'll call if you need anything?"

"Don't worry about me," Camille said, pulling the phone from her mouth so he couldn't hear the edges of her voice crack. "I'm tough."

***

Speeding east on the 210, Camille rode a headwind of smog to Monrovia. She'd taken the day off work to treat herself to a Green Street Chinese Chicken salad and some shoe shopping in Old

Town after the appointment, but now, all she could do was burn down the freeway and let her mind pale out.

Sprawled in front of her, Los Angeles was just a flat palm of land, open and calloused and grabbing. She'd been clutched within its suburbs her whole life, had felt the nag of consumption and perfection and heat clawing at her while she tried to fall asleep, searched for parking, or drifted the slick grocery aisles at Ralphs. Camille knew LA and her awkward place in it: she was a red-headed insurance agent driving the same dented Civic from college and the only vanity surgery she'd ever had was to remove her impacted wisdom teeth. Since she hadn't fixed her air conditioner, she kept the windows down, KROQ blaring, the wind laced with french fries and mariachi from the biodiesel van rattling in front of her as she followed the pull toward her mother's house.

Augusta was seventy-three, a retired elementary school secretary with a penchant for courtroom dramas and Swisher Sweets. Camille never felt comfortable with the fact that her mother smelled like a father, but Augusta waved her off, saying, "That way, people don't know I'm alone. They'll think some brute lives here, so they won't mess with me." When Camille was fifteen, her father had died of a heart attack in line at the bank while she was jumping hurdles at a track meet in Azusa. A middle-aged man dropping his checkbook on the marble floor, ballpoint pen rolling away, sweating and embarrassed as he roiled in a public place. Augusta never could bring herself to love another, so she didn't. She kept her diamond shined on her left hand and her husband's wedding band on a gold chain around her neck.

Camille parked in front of her childhood home, a low ranch-style house like all the others on the cul-de-sac. Crying in the front seat, she watched Augusta struggle out of the recliner and limp to the foyer.

"Cammy?" Augusta called from the screen door. "Why aren't you at work? What's wrong?"

Camille trembled, now red-faced in the street, waiting for the mailman to drive past. "I had a doctor's appointment to figure out why I've gained so much weight. It could just be a benign cyst in my uterus or maybe cancer. I go in for a scan tomorrow."

Augusta looked like a chipped white plate, but hobbled toward Camille and hugged her. "All right, take it easy and get in here."

They slid into their usual spots at the kitchen table. Augusta, a cutthroat strategist on eBay, collected salt-and-pepper shakers, the hutch cluttered with ceramic pairs—Santa and Rudolph, Lucy and Desi, a chicken and an egg. Camille moved two Dutch farm children as Augusta returned with glasses of Crystal Light and a bowl of Corn Nuts, nodding between crunches as Camille paraphrased the doctor's concerns.

"Don't kill yourself with worry," Augusta said. "This is scary business, but if something's in there, it's best to get rid of it now. Besides, of all the bad things we have in our family, cancer isn't one of them." She'd been just as straight-faced delivering her husband's eulogy.

"You're right," Camille said, inhaling the poker-night stink of her mother's shoulder.

"Best to face it head-on. No matter what this is, believe you're going to be fine." Augusta shuffled to the recliner, clutching her cedar humidor. "Hell, can you imagine how much worse this'd be if you had kids?" She cut a cigar. Two sparks flashed, a long gray exhale twisting out from her lips.

"What if I can't have them after this?"

"You've never mentioned it before."

"It'd be nice to have the choice."

Augusta funneled a handful of Corn Nuts. "This old broad desperately hoped you would, maybe even with Gage. But you're almost thirty-seven now and you haven't been living like you want kiddos, Cammy."

"Here we go."

"I'm not judging—I could barely handle one myself. But we've got to lay out all the facts here."

Augusta had hit that age when the insolence of time became more apparent with each visit. Her upper arms had melted wide and soft, while the waddle in her neck had loosened, her feet puffing over the tops of her thick flat sandals. Slumped in front of *Judge Judy,* Augusta's body was a daisy hunched with the last of its bloom.

"I hate to say it, but think of the timeline, sweets. You meet a guy, you date for a year, take a few months to plan the wedding, enjoy that newlywed life. Before you know it, you're over forty and those eggs are rotten."

"Christ, Mom. I have time."

Smoke cobwebbed across Augusta's face. "Life laughs loudest, right?"

***

The next day, Camille slid through the CT tube, praying she wouldn't have to poop. A low growl unwound inside, her stomach rioting without breakfast. It sounded like she'd hidden a guinea pig along for the ride. A guinea pig named Harriet. Camille bit the inside of her cheek, picturing the technician's surprise as four wee paws passed across his screen. Whenever her nervous laughter would leak out, her mother would hiss, "Pull it together, Camille!" and she imagined Augusta's reprimand on the slow slide through the scanner.

"Big inhale," the technician instructed.

Louder growls from her stomach as her eyes watered, a chuckle terrorizing her lips.

"Okay, I'm centering in on the area in question." The technician paused the machine to hover over Camille's abdomen. "Hold steady please?"

"Sorry."

A quick whir encircled her. Then it sounded like he reversed the scanner's direction. "Just one more time." The whir again. "All right, miss. You stay put while I get a second pair of eyes."

She listened to the soft swish of double-doors as he hurried out of the room.

Alone in the tube, her giggle vanished.

***

"Now count backward from ten."

Inhaling into the nasal tubes, Camille was prepped for what the doctor called "immediate mass-removal surgery." She breathed and breathed, eclipsing into a sunset of warm whiteness, a gauzy blue fluttering, the deep shush of gray. While Gage and Augusta paced the waiting room, Camille wondered where she would be when she awoke, until, blissed by oxygen, she just didn't care.

***

And the lights flared bright—azure, fuchsia, chartreuse—exquisite explosions behind her eyelids, a shadowsnap of color unfurling. The heat caught at Camille's forehead, dripping into her cheeks as she opened wide to swallow the morning sun. It ebbed through her, undulating, radiating.

"Is she awake?" Augusta asked.

"She seems happier sleeping," Gage said, his words a tiny tornado of truth whipping through the room.

***

Camille pried open her eyes, her lashes crusted together. As she dug out the gunk, she felt the tug of stitches below her navel and imagined black cord criss-crossing through her skin like a corset. She gagged. "Mom?"

"Hey, Cam," Augusta said, her face as ragged as those hobo clown paintings from the Rose Bowl flea market. She dabbed her cheeks. "How are you feeling?"

"Sore. Why are you crying?"

Gage rubbed Augusta's back as he approached the bed.

"What's wrong with me, Gage? Say it."

"They finished the surgery," he said, "and there's no cancer."

Camille exhaled. "That's great."

"The doctor said they found something else, though. That thing he felt at your appointment?"

"What, ovarian cyst?"

"No." Gage cleared his throat. "He called it a 'stone baby.' Three pounds. Like five months old."

"I had a baby?"

"Technically. Yes. But it passed away. And then calcified. In there."

Augusta shook her head, a quick sob slipping out.

"How long has it been in me?"

"A couple of years," Augusta said, dabbing again.

Camille turned to Gage, but he was blinking quickly, staring out the window.

"They say you're going to be just fine, Cammy," Augusta said, struggling to stand straight. The smile pinned to her face looked stolen.

"I want to see it."

***

An hour before discharge, a nurse wheeled Camille into a room halved by a blue privacy curtain. Camille focused on the rhythmic spin of the wheelchair crossing the floor. The nurse drew the curtain.

At the back of a room, a silver tray had been draped with a short sheet. Lumpy. Noiseless.

After locking Camille in place, the nurse pulled the tray closer to Camille. "Take your time. I'll be right outside."

Alone in the room, Camille waited for the door to shut. Then she reached out, lowering her fingers until she felt the thin cloth, slowly, the coolness tangible through the sheet. On the pier with Gage that night, a bay cruiser had pushed past them into the darkness, shearing the waves. Camille remembered the bow lights long after they'd passed. She pulled back the sheet.

It was mottled brown, like a mud-stained sneaker. Would it have toenails? Teeth? She picked it up. Dense, but soft. Cold. The head bulged while two birdlike legs dangled, thin and bent, the body covered in a gray lacework of veins. She had to be quick. Bending forward, her stitches straining, Camille used her free hand to tug the compression socks off her feet and style them into a mound under the sheet. With the sheet smoothed, she rolled the tray back behind the curtain. Then she tucked the baby, her baby, safely inside her gown.

***

Later that afternoon, Augusta and Camille sat exhausted and sweating at the rusted bistro table outside Camille's bungalow. A weed whacker buzzed next door, while clouds of gnats twirled between distilled rays of sun. Camille was relieved to be home, soaked in sunshine. They'd even done some gardening, the mulch fresh under their fingernails.

"Thanks, Mom. I really appreciate it."

Augusta mopped her forehead. "Never again."

"Honey, I'm home," Gage sang as he opened the backyard gate.

"Gage?" Augusta called, suddenly fresh and bright. "This is a surprise."

"Thought I'd stop by to welcome her home." He leaned in to hug Augusta and then kissed Camille's cheek. "Wow, you are remarkably sweaty, Cammy."

"Just enjoying my slice of paradise." She zeroed in on the white plastic bag in his hand. "Is that El Pollo Loco?"

"For m'lady." He handed her a three-piece chicken meal and gave Augusta a tostada salad. "And how're you feeling today?"

"Way better now."

Augusta stabbed some lettuce.

"What's up with the grubby-kid nails?" he asked, opening a half-chicken combo for himself. "You ladies do some gardening?"

"Against orders," Augusta muttered.

"What else am I supposed to do?" Camille asked, scraping dirt from her battered acrylics.

"I don't know," Gage said. "Sit there and wait for me to show up?"

Camille blushed. "And here you are."

"A true friend." He took another bite of his chicken leg. "What were you working on?"

Camille considered the dry curve of the pool, the desiccated bugs between the lounger slats. "Oh, just repotting. Fertilizing."

"Nice. Your birds turned out good." He walked over to her garden and then dragged his hand across the damp dirt. "You were right, they're beautiful all together."

"Yeah." Camille tried to smile, but her mouth felt tight, like a scab tearing. "C'mon, your chicken's getting cold."

Gage lowered his hand to steady himself, but it accidentally pushed through their newly smoothed dirt. He paused, then flicked some soil away. Then more.

"Gage, what are you looking for?" Augusta asked, standing up. "Let the birds be."

He dug faster and faster until his hand snapped back.

Camille shut her eyes, knowing what to expect: the shame, Gabe's rejection, a greedy news crew, maybe the tentative reach of a firefighter's hand. But before any of that, she imagined the click of a door, soft and safe, the life she'd really wanted, the glimmer of happiness brightest from the shadows.

REFRAIN

Snappy decided he could handle the quiet tingle of spring just this once. The grass around the baseball diamond was freshly cut, damp tufts heaped along its periphery, and beyond the outfield, azaleas were poised for spring, their buds a hopeful beacon in the bright Mardi Gras sun. Near the bleachers, fiddleheads waited to unfurl. A freckled blonde sprinted toward third base, ponytail swinging. It'd been years since he'd stopped by a high school game. According to the catcher's mother, the JV softball team was racking up more losses than wins this season, but Snappy didn't care. He'd shown up today, neat in his work clothes—shirt tucked, cap straight—and sat right there in the stands. Though he was tapping his foot, wrangling his thoughts from the dark place, he kept his hands out where everyone could see them. When another blonde went to bat, Snappy cheered as if he were someone's grandpa.

***

Two hours later, Snappy was back in the French Quarter, running scales at the piano before his Friday night set. The girls had lost by one run. A disappointment, certainly, but at least he wouldn't have to endure any celebratory bouncing and hugging, especially since the tendencies had slithered back into his life.

He'd stamped them down for so long. He was too old to throw away all his hard work.

Life was changing quickly enough to make him nervous. Last month, Snappy had come home to a notice shoved under his door. Evicted at the age of sixty-eight. At first, the news crushed him. His set-up had been ideal: cheap enough to afford with his gig money, hardly any palmetto bugs, and more than two thousand feet from a school. Then his cousin Bernard generously offered up their guest bedroom—half his current rent, with an invitation to stay as long as he wanted. But Bernard had a teenage daughter. Thirteen, flaxen-haired. Panicking, Snappy had claimed he didn't want to be a burden, but Bernard insisted. Let us help, he'd said. We've got room with Renee off at boarding school. Snappy had exiled himself from family for so long that he was scared to lose Bernard, his last connection to who he used to be. He'd been a good man once, before he screwed up. Bernard's offer to move in was what Snappy had been waiting for all these years: the chance to prove he'd changed, be the man he was supposed to be. All right, you got me, Snappy had said. And with a handshake, Snappy's usual defenses were razed. He was moving in.

"What's good, roomie?" Bernard asked, clutching his trumpet as he climbed the stage.

"Roomie, huh?" Snappy whistled. "Bet you never thought you'd be saying that at your age."

"You moving in's a happy lagniappe. Nothing more important than family."

Snappy made sure he smiled. Two years ago, he had stopped at the library to take advantage of the free internet. Not having a computer at home kept him honest, but he wasn't immune to temptation, so on a day when the library wasn't crowded and the urges were about to boil over, Snappy forced himself to browse local jazz gigs as a distraction. A post for the DuPont Quartet had interested him not only because it sounded like the perfect fit, but because his last name was also DuPont. Five emails later, Bernard asked if he happened to know a Charlotte DuPont. Snappy said yes, his mother. Snappy and Bernard were second cousins.

They met for scotch before the audition. Bernard was in his forties and thankfully too young to have grown up enduring Sunday suppers at Auntie Amelia's. Charlotte's oldest sister Amelia was a terrible cook who doled out shade along with her succotash each week. And once she'd slugged her after-dinner brandy, Auntie would trawl up all the times she'd been personally wronged, like when a teenaged Charlotte had goosed her into Lake Pontchartrain or when Snappy's daddy left "to work the mines" in Virginia ("Or work that street piece Virginia," she'd slur). Auntie Amelia tended to these injustices every week, ensuring they thrived and blossomed larger than her own life. And because Amelia let them live rent-free downstairs, Charlotte endured her penance like it was just an old dandelion she couldn't stamp down.

Bernard had been born after Auntie passed, so he'd never been forced to go swamping through the family lore. He simply took Snappy for what he was: the only other guy left standing in a very short bloodline.

"You all packed now?" Bernard asked.

"Indeed. My box is taped up and ready to go."

"Just one?"

Realizing how pathetic that sounded, Snappy spruced it up with a lie. "The rest is in storage until I can sell it."

Bernard nodded and then buzzed his lips. "To be honest, I'm glad to have some testosterone around, especially with Renee visiting this weekend."

Snappy felt his hands tense. "Oh yeah?"

"She's back for Mardi Gras, so she'll be lurking about with her new bad attitude. Wait 'til you get a load of her."

Snappy swallowed. He'd banked on her being tucked away in a dorm room most of the year, maybe returning home for an uncomfortable week at Christmas when he could hide in his room under the guise of "giving them family time." But her surprise arrival stung like a falling buck moth. "Should be a treat."

"It'll be something, all right," Bernard muttered. With their set about to start, he nodded at the drums and bass and then faced the crowd. "Welcome to N'awlins everyone," he said into the mic, drawling it out for the tourists. "We're the DuPont Quartet with the soundtrack for your Mardi Gras fun. Laissez les bon temps rouler!"

As a pack of college boys whooped from their barstools, Snappy stretched his fingers a good octave and a half. Though the rest of his body might've quietly initiated the dust-to-dust process, his hands were as strong as ever, the pink scars looping around his knuckles, a history he couldn't hide. Fingers that meaty were more common on baseball catchers, bricklayers, maybe a clumsy foreman. But at the keys, his hands were magic. At the keys, he could be free.

Snappy pressed down while Bernard leaned back, letting his trumpet moan. Brush of snare, pluck of double bass. Then the cycles, the waiting, a melody bone sure in all four of them. Everyone in the pocket.

"Turn it out, Snappy," his old bassist had hollered back in the day, his hands ricocheting between octaves. The nickname stuck. And with it, the welcomed chance to become someone else.

***

After his Friday night sets, Snappy liked to wind down with a Pernod at his kitchen table. It felt right in New Orleans, an indulgence for an old man. From the wrinkled droop of his paunch to his concave chest, he was officially on the other side of the fence now. Snappy needed to moisten his lips before he ate or spoke, found he had to inquire about the spiciness anytime andouille popped up in the gumbo. Yet there was pride in his chords: for his talent, of course. But also for making it this far without any other slip-ups.

He surveyed his apartment for the last time. He didn't have much, mostly because he hadn't stayed in one place long enough. Scrambling out of Georgia at twenty-four, he'd left a note to his mother on a sheet of staff paper claiming that the heat had become too much to bear. For years, he'd drifted down the southeastern corridor, a feather whirling in the wind, crashing in hot-sheet motels while he rustled up paychecks playing cotillions, the second floor at Nordstrom, and once, memorably, a purity ball.

Katrina had blown the city open for him, the fury of water and wind more of a rebirth than a displacement. When he showed up a year after her wrath, rents and hopes were still soggy. The Crescent City felt like a pocket someone had emptied out. Or maybe an opportunity. For once in his life, he'd wanted to stay. He could hit the keys every day and pick up gigs, letting music be his distraction. He'd force a quiet life, nestled in the eye of the storm.

Snappy zipped his old duffle bag. It was in good shape after all this time. Twenty years ago, on his first sojourn through New Orleans, Snappy had let himself fall in love. Simple, good love. Val was a fifth-grade teacher, also in her forties, a woman who'd tossed thousands of pennies in the old Gumbel Fountain, wishing for a man who'd give up pastrami with her during Lent and compliment her gold velvet coat during the Christmas sparkle of Reveillon. After six months of dating, she'd gifted him a green nylon bag. Pack your stuff, come live with me, she'd said. We can make it feel new, just the two of us. They'd both realized it was a step closer to making it official at the courthouse.

The day before he was supposed to sign the lease, he took her to breakfast and told her he'd cheated on her. A lie, of course. He could picture composing for her until his hands gave out. But there was one thing he couldn't share. And when she'd handed him the duffel bag, he knew it was too late. He'd have to protect her.

Val had sobbed for an hour at the table, her eggs and boudin hardening on her plate while all the women in the restaurant glared at him, this son of a bitch who made a lady cry in public. Then she smoothed her hair, claiming that she could forgive him, they were all human, she'd even fantasized about her ex-boyfriend Germaine once. Snappy considered the pleading pull of her eyes, the shiny St. Michael's medallion around her neck. Yet his gut burned with the truth: you get one lie with a good woman, and he'd already blown his. He never let himself love again.

But he'd been loved once.

***

The next morning, the lure of a JV double-header urged Snappy out of the Marigny and across Decatur, through the French Quarter. He knew he shouldn't go, that three hours at another softball game was just too much temptation, but he promised himself he would leave if he couldn't behave.

Bourbon Street was still sluicing the previous night's mistakes, a burn of plastic-bottled vodka and horse piss cutting the spring breeze. Half the tourists, destroyed by hangovers, were propped up around the sugar-dusted tables at Cafe du Monde, while everyone else had already jump-started the day. A pair of identical twins sported colossal feather and rhinestone headdresses that bounced as they sauntered through the crowd and posed for photos. From a balcony, a woman in a gold tinsel wig ground down, the brutalities of motherhood revealed like bobcat swipes around her navel. Below her, tourists in tuxedo T-shirts chugged from go-cups and howled, while a bachelorette party in Saints jerseys and flashing neon necklaces held hands as they snaked along the sidewalk. A man with one shoe shuffled behind a wheelchair, pushing a sleeping bulldog.

As Snappy tried to sidle through the crowd, someone towered by on stilts. A black bodysuit, red hourglass across the chest, eight hairy limbs attached to the back. The figure twisted to face him, slowly smelling him. Then one of the long hairy limbs stretched and tickled Snappy on the nape. Terrified of spiders, Snappy felt his heart quicken, and when a horn blasted behind him, he lost his footing.

"Mind your step now, pal."

Snappy turned to find Bernard smiling, trumpet in hand.

"Could've been a helluva nosedive," Bernard said, considering a nearby puddle of vomit, the damp hem on Snappy's pants. "Promise you shower before coming over?"

"Might need more than that at this rate," Snappy said.

A cheerleader sashayed over twirling a magenta boa. "Who dat, daddy!"

Snappy thrilled at the moniker, but kept a respectable public distance as he led her in a waltz. "Pardon me while I feel like a young man again," he called to Bernard.

Bernard laughed as she spun away. "What're you up to today?"

Instinctively, Snappy tucked his hands in his pockets. "Just getting after one last muffuletta before I head your way."

"Delicious. Hey, you want to come by my house around six? Patricia's setting up a big boil. We can pinch some tails tonight before the krewes pop off tomorrow."

"You got it," Snappy said, dodging the spider guy's return.

"Heads up, Renee's got a friend staying with us this week. The teen angst is code red."

Snappy tried not to flinch. Two teenage girls. He forced a smile. "Good to know."

"'Til then, coz."

Bernard hot stepped down the street with his trumpet held high, its gold bell glinting like a refurbished halo.

***

Muffuletta in hand, Snappy squeezed onto a park bench. Next to him, a ragged woman in a fox stole hummed and swayed, sipping a frozen daiquiri. Snappy quietly unwrapped his sandwich, hoping to ignore her and the thick foxtail jabbing his bread.

"Got an extra bite for me, gramps?" she asked.

"Sure enough." Irritated, he handed her the smallest of his sandwich quarters. "These damn things could end me," she mumbled.

A family with three daughters bent toward the fountain. Snappy struggled to keep his eyes on his sandwich. "Be the perfect way to go, though."

As they chewed, a bird landed at their feet. White and rangy, it was runtier than the herons around town, but flaunted an immense wingspan. It studied him with hot red eyes.

"Where y'at?" Snappy asked.

The bird's black-capped head turned, questioning and quick. It was missing two talons. "Usually's a June bird," the woman said, a tumble of sesame seeds and olive chunks bouncing off the fox head onto the concrete.

"Maybe he's lost."

She tossed some crust. "You came early, huh?"

The bird pecked around Snappy's loafer.

"Get gone," Snappy said, shaking his shoe at it.

Then the woman held out a pinch of ham. Snatching it, the bird scrambled up and across Snappy's moon-pale foot, struggling for balance as it chewed, claws razoring deep into his exposed skin. Snappy heard himself yelp. As the welts throbbed, he surprised himself by bashing the bird's thin wing backward.

"Stop it! Stop yourself!" the woman yelled. Several people came over to gawk.

Screeching, the bird puffed up to full size. Snappy jumped back, frightened by its hidden strength.

MOUTH

"Jesus, man. You never been hungry?"

The bird toppled to the ground beak first with a cracking sound more hollow than Snappy expected.

"What's the matter with you?" someone yelled.

"I didn't mean to. It just happened." Snappy panicked. He'd never registered in the database, something that could immediately end him if any cops caught up with him. Stretching wide, the bird flared a twisted wing and strained upward, a sweep of white lurching crooked across the turquoise sky.

"I swear," Snappy said to the angry crowd. "I don't know where that came from."

The old woman stared him down. "I see you," she growled, daiquiri juice clinging to her face like misplaced kisses.

***

The St. Charles streetcar left the French Quarter and rambled Uptown along the dusty track, past the gaudy fluorescence of pizzerias and auto parts stores, toward more revelry and the old columned history near Bernard's. Snappy, jammed onto a seat with his box, the duffle bag, and a sack of sweets, sat nervously in a sea of elbows and rear ends. He'd barely escaped that park situation, could've been outed in a heartbeat. He tried shifting his focus to the craggy oaks muddling the sunset. Throws glittered down, jeweling the evening. His foot burned.

Snappy disembarked into another boozy crowd, the Garden District rollicking. He followed the other passengers to neutral ground, careful not to brush up against anyone. Only when he hit the wide leafy canopies of Prytania Street could he relax. He hobbled past the water-wrecked marble and moldy poetry of Lafayette Cemetery. So much damn death in New Orleans. It spooked him. Not that he had a will. Casket, oven, wouldn't make a difference when it was all over. Before Charlotte's passing, Snappy hadn't spoken with his mother in decades, couldn't tell if her disappointment or his shame would be worse. Once she died, he'd been too humiliated to pay his respects. So it'd probably be Bernard and the guys coming by to play an old man off the stage. Had he lived his life the way he wanted? He limped across the street, past the tailgaters. Had anyone?

It'd happened just once, he reminded himself. A moment forever teetering like a teapot on a table's edge. The worst summer to hit Georgia in years, smothering like a hand across the mouth. August had been stilted with irritation, the desperate whir of parlor fans. Snappy was twenty-four, unmarried, still living at home. Clara sat at the piano refusing to play her scales, thirteen and indolent.

"We've been at this for weeks," Snappy had said. "Why should I teach you anything new if you're never going to get past this?"

"I don't want to do it." Clara got up from the piano and pouted in front of the French doors. Sunshine illuminated the holes in her eyelet dress, the outline of a training bra.

"You don't have a choice," Snappy said. "Your mama paid through the month."

"This is stupid."

"We've only got a few minutes left," he said. "The sooner we do this, the sooner you can leave." Snappy patted the bench next to him. "Come on, now. Be sweet."

MOUTH

Clara rolled her eyes. As she returned to the bench, strands of blonde hair slipped from her braid and cascaded over her freckled shoulders.

"There you go," he said.

She laid her hands on the black keys. Snappy stood behind her and positioned his fingers on top of hers, bringing both sets to the white keys. His hands were unblemished. "Like this."

"Fine."

When he sat next to her, he noticed her legs were crossed at the ankles, pink sandals dangling above the pedals. "Undo your legs a bit?" He placed his hand lightly on her thigh, her skin smooth and cool below his sweaty palm. She'd apparently started shaving since their last lesson. "You have to press the pedals."

"Okay already."

"No, do it right." Snappy's hands skimmed down her calf and put her feet directly on the brass pedals. He'd thought about her a lot that summer.

Clara stiffened. "I got it." She pounded the keys, the tips of her sandals dangling over the pedals.

"Remember the legs." Snappy pushed her knee as a reminder about the pedals, but once he touched her soft skin, his hand wanted nothing more than to wander. So he let it, slowly, up her thigh, until he reached the cotton elastic of her underwear.

***

Bernard owned one of those old Garden District homes off Prytania, a gated Victorian more beat down than the others on the block, but majestic compared to Snappy's weathered shack.

It'd been in Bernard's family for decades, the wainscoting cracking as if the gnarled fingers of his forefathers were still holding tight. Snappy tucked his shirt in.

Based on the way Bernard stayed late chatting up the crowd every Friday night, Snappy often forgot he had a family and a nine-to-fiver. This whole other life, a household of females and work deadlines and familial duty. It made him jealous, but mostly curious, like looking into the warm glow of a neighbor's window on a brisk winter night.

Snappy tried the gate but it was stuck, and after several yanks, it screeched open. He carefully squeezed past, unable to shove it completely shut, and then climbed the steps to Bernard's front door. A purple and green feather wreath adorned the knocker, a fancy reminder he'd be in the presence of ladies soon enough. He hoped he wasn't sweating and rang the bell.

"Edmund," Patricia sang as she opened the door. "So lovely to see you again."

"Thank you for having me, ma'am."

A garlicky waft crested over him in the entryway, clashing with an undertow of something sweet. He glanced around, sticking close to the door.

"Still so formal? You're family. Make yourself at home."

He set the box and duffle bag down and then pulled a dozen pralines out of the sack. "I also stopped off at Southern Candymakers. Figured why not enjoy the tourist life today?" The foyer smelled inviting, like fresh sugar cookies. But Patricia would've baked a more elaborate dish. He inhaled again. A backpack sat on the countertop, olive green and pinned with buttons, clichéd hexes on authority.

"Hey roomie," Bernard called from the bar cart. "What're we drinking tonight?"

"Too early for scotch?"

"Hell no." Bernard poured two fingers of Dewar's. "You limping?"

Snappy had wrapped his foot with a long cloth bandage, hoping to make the burning stop. It hadn't worked. "Not my proudest moment, but I got attacked by a bird this afternoon."

"A baby bird brought down a big dude like you?"

"I'm a sensitive guy."

As they laughed and drank, Renee skulked into the kitchen with another girl trailing next to her, both in denim miniskirts and glittery eye masks. Their inky black hairstyles were a trend among high schoolers—half the outfielders sported the same dye jobs. Only their eyebrows revealed their natural hair color, a honeyed blond.

"Renee, meet your cousin, Edmund."

"In a sec," she said, fixated on her cell phone.

"Don't be rude."

"Fine. Hey."

She certainly seemed like a little bitch, which would help quiet the roar. "Good to meet you." Snappy sounded too loud. "And welcome back. How's school?"

"Totally lame."

Patricia frowned. "Come on."

"What? It's true."

"Things will get better," Patricia said.

"When?"

"College," Snappy said. "Nothing like being young and dumb. Except maybe getting away with it."

Renee smiled. "At least you're honest."

"I told you," Bernard said. "Respect your elders, Renee. They've been around."

"Tori, are you going to introduce yourself?" Patricia asked.

The tips of Tori's hair had been dipped pink, like she'd gotten caught reaching into a cotton candy machine. The mask electrified her green eyes. "Hi." She smelled heavily of vanilla.

"Glad to meet you, Tori," Snappy said. "You enjoying your Mardi Gras?"

"Sure, not partying with our friends is a fabulous fucking time," Renee said.

Patricia didn't flinch at the language or the sentiment. "You don't need to hang out with seventeen-year-olds."

"Let's get out of here," Renee barked to Tori. Both girls grabbed their phones and hustled toward the backyard.

"Thirteen going on twenty-six," Bernard murmured.

Snappy was sweating. "Don't envy you at all."

Bernard shook his head. "Want to hear my new Cannonball record? Used vinyl from Japan. Got it for eighty bucks."

"That'd be fine."

They walked down a hallway lined with Renee's school portraits. Baby ringlets gave way to long flaxen elementary-school strands. And now, the surly dyed rebellion of eighth grade.

Bernard stood next to him and considered the photos. "She used to be so sweet. It's like, what happened?"

***

MOUTH

In the dining room, crawfish and corncobs steamed on the table. Snappy kept his hands folded in his lap while the girls sat across from him, their smirks as wide as the gold masks they were still wearing.

Patricia glared at them. "Really?"

Renee shrugged. "It's Mardi Gras."

Bernard and Patricia both made the sign of the cross and bowed their heads, while Renee rolled her eyes at Tori. Snappy smiled at them.

"Bless us O Lord, for these thy gifts, which we are about to receive, from thy bounty, through Christ our Lord. Amen."

"Praise be, Jesus," Renee drawled. Tori snickered.

"Glad you didn't have children, Snappy?"

Snappy never could figure out a response to those kinds of comments, so he defaulted to a laugh. "Everything looks delicious, ma'am."

"Thank you. Help yourself."

Tabasco rose from the crawfish, making his eyes water. "Smells like this has some heat?"

"Good for the soul," Patricia said, winking.

It'd be too spicy for him, he could smell it, but he grabbed the tongs anyway. His hands, unwieldy with such delicate servingware, slipped, causing a cob to roll across the table.

"Shit." Anxiety slicked across Snappy's forehead. "Pardon my salty talk." He dabbed at the orange stain forming on the runner.

"How'd you get that giant scar?" Renee asked, pointing to his left hand.

"This?" He tried to stay nonchalant as he mopped his forehead. "Just got too quick with my hands once."

Renee frowned. "Nasty."

"Hey, can you be sweet for once?" Bernard asked.

Snappy grinned, seizing the opportunity to deflect. "She's right, it's ugly. But it's a good forty years old."

"Did it hurt?" Tori asked.

He nodded, sucking on a crawfish. "Bernard, can I bother you for another scotch?"

"Never a bother."

With a few more sips, Snappy would feel the slow roll of scotch coming in. He could handle it.

"You know, I have wanted to ask you about that big old thing," Bernard said, refilling his glass. "The best stories leave the worst scars."

"Then you're about to be disappointed."

"Come on, try us."

Most people were too polite to ever ask about it, but just in case, Snappy had a backup story ready. He took a long pull of scotch. "Really, it was just a dog bite. Nothing more exciting than that."

***

After the boil, the girls scrolled through their phones until Patricia sighed. "If you can't act like adults, go upstairs."

"We're not adults."

"Well you're not babies either. Go."

They sprinted up the stairs, granting Snappy the chance to relax into conversation while Patricia cut the King Cake.

MOUTH

"The bride was real country," Snappy said, chuckling about the worst wedding he'd ever played. "So nervous, she passed gas right there on the altar. Never smelled anything like that from a human. Clocked you like rotten oysters." He bit into the cake, hitting something hard.

"Is it you?" Bernard asked.

Snappy nodded, pulling a plastic figurine from his mouth. "I got the baby." He wiped it off and held it up for everyone.

Patricia poured his coffee, giggling. She tapped her upper lip.

"What?" Snappy yanked the napkin from his collar and then wiped his mouth.

"You're making it worse, man," Bernard said. "Go take care of that."

"All right. But hands off my cake." Snappy tucked the figurine into his pocket as he lumbered upstairs, mopping his face with his cuff. As usual, he turned left and opened the guest bathroom door.

"Get out!"

He jolted as the door slammed shut. "Sorry. I didn't mean to interrupt. I'm sorry."

Tori burst out, storming past him and into the bedroom.

"I didn't see anything," he said. Her panties were lavender. He waited, heart pounding.

The corridor smelled sweet, like buttercream.

"Hello?" she called.

"Yes?" Snappy said.

"Why are you hiding out there?"

He stepped closer to find Tori on the bed in her temporary room, her gold mask strewn across the nightstand. "I wanted to be respectful."

"Okay."

He nodded, making sure his feet were firmly on the carpet outside her bedroom, sweaty hands behind his back. "Where's Renee?"

"Snuck out to meet some guy. Whatever." She'd removed her combat boots. Her pedicure was pink, chipped like no one had told her she needed to maintain it.

Snappy swallowed and stepped into the room with his hands in his pockets, his fingers clutching the plastic figurine. "Are you having fun?"

"No. Are you?"

"I was having a fine time."

"I'm bored out of my mind."

His shirt was growing damp and he could hear Bernard and Patricia filling the sink with water. But that scent. So light, so sweet. Like he could rest his tongue against it. "You've got your book. That'll help pass the time."

"I guess."

"Depends on what you're reading, of course. Has to be good." Snappy sat next to her on the bed, the chenille soft under his palms. "What've you got?"

She stiffened and reluctantly handed him an old pulp paperback.

"Wow, I haven't read one of these since the sixties," he said.

"I collect them."

It was her lip gloss. Candy corn, no, vanilla frosting, he could taste it already. "Then you must be an old soul." He began reading aloud:

> *They lay on the beach. The Hawaiian sun felt warm on their skin, but a breeze from the palm trees cooled them. Doris listened to the crashing waves, the gulls swirling overhead.*
> *"This is paradise," she whispered.*
> *"No," John said. "You are." He kissed her.*

Snappy shut the book, the tendencies roiling. "Don't tell me you believe this garbage, do you?"

Tori blushed. "I like it."

"Why?"

As she shrugged, he snuck a glance at the creamy stretch of her legs.

"Makes me feel like I'm somewhere else. Or someone else," she said.

"You've got a whole lifetime to be in love."

She rolled her eyes. "That's only in movies."

"Not necessarily. I've been in love before."

"And was it like that?" she asked, nodding at the book.

"Not exactly. But it can make you do crazy stuff."

They sat on the bed in silence, though he felt like he was panting.

"What kind of dog was it?" she asked.

Snappy glanced down at the shiny white scars, the molar-shaped indentations. He put his hands in his pockets. The figurine felt cool in his palm. "She was just a pup. It's hard to get mad at something so small."

Tori nodded.

"Do you have any scars?" he asked.

"Yeah. One."

"No, you're too pretty for a scar."

She peeked over his shoulder toward the door. "I was, like, seven."

"How'd it happen?"

Tori studied the book cover. "It doesn't matter."

"Sure it does." The old ache wailed inside him. Snappy could hear Patricia rinsing pans downstairs, figured Bernard must be shuttling wine glasses to the counter. There was a long table of dishes to be washed. He angled his body to keep Tori in the room. "It's okay. You can tell me."

"I don't want to." She tied on the mask, her leg bouncing. "It's secret."

"Can you show me?"

"Snappy," Bernard called from the base of the stairs. "Did you fall in?"

As Snappy's fingers trembled inside his pocket, he let go of the figurine. "I can keep a secret."

Tori froze, her green eyes wide behind the mask. Bernard was coming up the stairs, steady footfalls. But Snappy was so close. All those years of hiding, denying. He reached out and watched his hand drift up her thigh.

"Snappy? What are you doing?"

"Nothing." Snappy raised his hands above his head.

Tori shook.

"Why's she so upset? Tori, you okay?"

She covered her face.

"What the hell happened?" Bernard asked Snappy.

Snappy felt sick. "We were just talking."

Tori scurried into the closet. Bernard crouched near her. "What's wrong, honey?"

"I only came in to chat," Snappy pleaded.

"Him," she whispered. "Up my leg."

Bernard faced him, something gray and sharp hardening behind his eyes.

"C'mon, she's just a kid," Snappy said. "Why would I do that?"

Bernard turned to Tori again, handed her a tissue. Then he slowly stood. "That the kind of man you are?"

"Bernard, I'm family," Snappy said.

"I let you into my house. My home."

"Uncle Jojo, come beat some ass," Tori bawled into her phone. "Hurry."

Snappy flushed cold. Too quickly, hip bones cracking, he mustered all his strength into his shoulder, an old move he remembered from his senior year of high school football, and heaved past. When Bernard struck him between the shoulder blades, Snappy lurched and was already winded by the time he hit the stairs, but he struggled down as fast as his arthritic knees would go, his grip slipping.

"Edmund? Bernie!" Patricia called as Snappy rushed past her. "What's going on?"

Tori gripped the banister. "You're fucking dead. They're coming for you," she screamed down. "You're a dead man."

But I'm not, Snappy thought, slipping on a throw rug in the foyer. He'd been loved once; he'd touched it. As he stumbled into the night, Bernard closing in behind him, Snappy's chest heaved. He closed his eyes, too fatigued to go on, old and clinging to a rusted gate he wasn't strong enough to shut. And when Bernard knocked him to the ground, the heel of his loafer cracking each of Snappy's fingers, Snappy couldn't help but claw, out, away, still mistaking the darkness for peace.

JENNY

Everyone begins in darkness. Rippling from a quiet explosion, we all bound forward into the unknown. And we wait—though we're terrible at waiting—while time and water and luck churn to make us bigger, stronger, more complete, until we wail into this world, lungs terrified as we leave the life aquatic. Somehow, we adapt. Stand, walk, run. Grass to dirt to dust.

But not for me. The wail continued. A low thrumming in the ear, a whisper whirlpooling inside the conch. *Dive in, go back.*

Take one look at this glittering tail to see just how ready I am.

***

My routine steadies me. First, I set the space heater to seventy-seven degrees and clip a travel fan to the toilet paper holder. Once the bathroom feels balmy, I scatter the tub with fistfuls of landscaping sand.

After that, I need a solid ten minutes to ease into the bathtub. It's not easy maneuvering alone. I'm built like a seal, though not as lithe. Add the athletic bandages swathing me thigh to ankle, plus two yards of seafoam green tulle layered around that, and I can't rush. But oh, the luxury in limitation. Once I'm situated, there's nothing to do but admire my long sparkling practice tail. Sapphire dorsal, turquoise underside. And two scalloped clam shells giving my chest its best life. There I am, glittering under the wan bathroom light. Alone, but illuminated. The real me, without acne-pitted cheeks or springtime allergies or a reliance on my feet to get around. In the water, I am ablaze.

My real tail has been hanging in the bedroom closet for the past year like the promise of a wedding dress. And, like a bride, I haven't shown anyone what's inside the garment bag yet. Instead, I've been elbow-deep in sequins most evenings, stitching glittering scales into a pattern inspired by parrotfish. I knocked out the final row last night, only to find myself in tears. It's all within reach.

On days when I feel like I'm nothing more than a slug sliming across a straw doormat, I slip into my tail and flap gently in front of my bedroom mirror. Maybe rest my hands on my hips, posing like the Jenny Haniver nailed above my bed. To most people, Jenny's just an old, dried stingray, folded to look like a seductress with a tail. Kitsch from a bygone era, a lie hand-fashioned by sailors hoping to impress loved ones once they returned home. But to me, she's more than that. The impossible made possible, she always says. A lighthouse marking my horizon, assuring me that I'm close. So close.

With an indulgent flick, like I'm taunting an armada, I slip under.

***

Truth be told, I've never seen the ocean. Born and bred on a sunflower farm outside Topeka, I know all about the choking expanse of earth and sky. The curse of solitude and land. I know exactly how you can suffocate from too much air.

Though the day-to-day of my life is swept up in the concrete tsunami of Los Angeles, the very beach I dream of just a quick drive away, I've never once touched the sand. And I've been here in Culver City three years now. Instead, I let gridlock and hookah bars and rundown donut shops be a breakwater against the reality I've been too scared to face. Because what if it's not as good as I imagined? Or worse, what if it is?

My roommate has no idea I mermaid. Marie and I met when, in a boldness fueled by some fancy Chardonnay a client had gifted me, I advertised my spare bedroom online, hopeful I'd make a new friend. Marie was the only one who responded to my ad. When we met for boba, she showed up with a Big Gulp and said, "It'll be more of a crash pad situation, you know?" I appreciated that. It's not often people show you who they really are.

I've never had roommates. Never had a ton of close friends either and that didn't change once I moved out here. Socializing in LA dries me up. Maybe it's the unrelenting sunshine that exhausts me. Or the lazy-mouthed speech, fried and perpetually questioning, . . . *riiiiiiight???*, even the most mundane conversations mushing out like you've stepped in freshly chewed gum. I tense with every *What do you do?*, these conversations never about an actual interest in my job but quick career calculations, what they might get from me, who I could introduce them to. Which is why I thought having a roommate would deliver a built-in friend. Or at least bridge the gulf of my loneliness. It hasn't, but thankfully I've got Laurel, my lovely Laurel, who electrified my sea the minute I walked into her toy store.

I mean, talk about fate. I live a pretty quiet life doing toy voiceovers, mostly for babies. The playmat where the golden-haired princess pops up to yodel the alphabet? That's me. Or the buck-toothed dragon plushie that giggles when you squish its belly? Yup, me again. The royalties fund my sequins and waterproofing. But recording in the studio every month is more than that. I'm alive when I'm drenched in the spotlight of that dank recording booth, my voice a north star. Of course, the minute I step out of the booth, I'm nobody again. But every time Maya, my favorite soundie, equalizes me to perfection, I matter. And that's enough to make me want to keep mattering.

I'd stopped by the toy store one random Wednesday two years ago to listen to my work on Karissa the Peppermint Fairy, but found myself drawn to Laurel's gravelly voice instead.

"Welcome," she'd said, eating a popsicle as I popped in. "Cute sunglasses."

"Target," I'd replied, too struck by her smile to pretend they were designer.

"Target has good shit."

I blushed as I beelined to the pink toddler section, squatting to the bottom shelf so my face could cool off. But then she was standing next to me.

"New baby in the family? Niece?"

"No way. Sorry, I mean no, I don't have any babies to buy for. Just trying to find myself. My voice. I'm a voiceover artist."

"Badass." Which is not something I'd ever been called. She gestured to the fairy I was holding. "Are you in there?"

I raised an eyebrow. "Find out for yourself."

Laurel picked up Karissa, flicked the button, and closed her eyes as Karissa trilled about candy. "There you are." And we both laughed. Isn't that just like life? A sneaker wave knocking you over while you stare at the sunset.

Laurel. My mountain. She's the kind of woman who finds peace backpacking through Joshua Tree. Who pushes her limits pounding dirt trails and asphalt running marathons. She's happiest under the sun, potting echeveria on a Saturday afternoon. I'm hoping she'll be more than just a friend. She hasn't been out to my house yet because rush hour between her place in the Valley and mine gets vile, so we try to meet somewhere halfway for vegan food. But after my big reveal, I bet she'll be more of a fixture around here. Hugging me in the foyer. Sipping rosé while we roast seaweed before dinner. Us.

Until then, Marie's been working out okay. Though I do have to endure the sounds of her midnight intimacies, especially with her latest hookup, a woman I've dubbed The Moaner. Cranking my headphones mostly tunes out Marie's romantic escapades. But not with The Moaner. There's a lot of whimpering and purring, like a kitten sniffing her first catnip. I try not to let it get me lonely by reminding myself it's just part of my unspoken deal with Marie: I don't inquire about the many women who stay over, she never questions me about all the Sea Spray candles nooked around the house.

I haven't told anyone about my tail or refurbished waterbed or the plywood trunk that I bedazzled as a treasure chest. Not because I'm ashamed. I've just been dreaming of this life for so long that it needs to be perfect when it arrives. I sped west from the heartland, leaving my mom and sister in order to create my own heartland, and as much as I want to shine my crazy like a pearl to be admired, it has to be with the right person. Someone who makes me feel less alone. I've been a shadow chasing the moonlight of my own life for so long—I just want to be the light. And when I'm with Laurel, I gleam.

"Nora, what's with all the sand in the tub?" Marie asked as I passed her in the hallway the other night.

I'd just applied a nourishing seaweed mask, my forehead, cheeks, and, if she'd peeked under my nightshirt, my entire torso, reborn green and slick. Nervous my shirt would stick to my body and out me, I kept moving. "I planted some gladiolas in the backyard."

She glanced out at the yellowed stalks, the reefs of dry dirt. "Then where are the flowers?"

"Soon," I said, drifting toward my bedroom. "A blossom like that takes time."

***

"I *wUV* you just the way you are!"

Maya shakes her head and buzzes in. "Remember, this is for toddlers."

Nodding, I step back from the mic and breathe with my diaphragm, prepping to launch my voice even higher. I like to think I keep getting booked because I know which toymakers want *TEE-hee* and which ones prefer *tee-HEE*. I never meet my clients. They just blindly follow my voice. Got to be a compliment in there somewhere.

"I *WUv* you just the way you are!"

Maya gives me a thumbs-up. "Next?"

My highlight reel boasts of natural articulation, a smooth German accent, and the ability to sound like a toddler.

"Oopsie-daisy willie-waisy!"

"You're killing it, Nora."

I squeeze tighter, throwing more weight into my pitch. "Will you be my fwiend 'til the vewy end?"

Laurel's name flashes on my phone.

"I gotta take this, Maya," I say, scrambling out of the booth. "Soft ten?"

"Right now? Who is it?"

Shhh, a good friend, I mouth.

"Tell your girlfriend to stop cutting into your recording time," she calls, and I delight at her mistake.

"Your mom says hi," I whisper, sailing past.

She throws a foam mic cover at my back as I buzz out into the alley. I head toward a quiet spot between recycling bins.

"Rise and shine, Nora!" Laurel says.

How I cannot wait until she's murmuring those very words from my pillow someday. "I was just thinking about you," I say.

"Must be fate 'cause Cherise popped in early to finish inventory at the store today. Want to sneak out for coffee? I'm dragging."

"Late night?" I ask, my jealousy already bared like piranha teeth.

Laurel laughs. "Caffeine first."

A rat scuttles through the flattened veggie boxes. I surprise myself by rooting down harder onto the dirty pile.

"Be there in fifteen," I muster.

***

My mind races as I walk to her work, cataloging every friend and cousin she could've been out with. Maybe she had to stay late to unload a new shipment. Or maybe it was simply insomnia. I continue to spiral until I'm standing on the curb in front of the toy store, and she greets me with two cappuccinos. She smells solid and earthy, like hands that recently dug out basil. I want those hands in my hair.

"Yes, please." I take a sip.

"Feel like taking a drive?" she asks. "I need a fresh scene."

"We can go get my car washed," I say, incorporating voice restraint techniques I use on frustrating jobs.

"Perfect."

My heart sharks inside me. We pick up my car behind the studio, heading out on the 405 for three exits, and then get off on the one aisled with pink freeway azaleas, which I mentally note for my future bouquet list. There's a drive-thru car wash that's half-price on weekdays and empty after the morning rush hour. Since being landbound is a burden I must bear right now, I try to make the most of it. I show up every other Tuesday at ten, like it's not the best part of my week. As if I simply baby my shitty old Jetta. Esmerelda from the dry crew hollers my name and waves.

"Exactly how often do you come here?" Laurel asks.

A briny need to reveal everything—the tail, my heart—swells inside me. But I swallow it down.

"Enough to keep it tight and right," I say, tapping my cracked dashboard.

Laurel laughs. "Clearly."

Anxiety shimmers through me as I pull up to the menu to select a wash. I've never done this in front of someone else. My go-to is The Clean Supreme because that level of spray is the most oceanic. But now, with a heap of animatronic queen heads littering the floor and Laurel smiling right next to me, it's like my period barged in while I'm sporting white jeans. I drop it into neutral and let my car roll forward. Soon we're awash in the coolness, the windshield water-blurred. I relax.

"So what've you been up to?" I ask. My hand rests on the center console, inches from her hip.

"I officially started dating someone two weeks ago!" The smile that slows across her face makes my stomach plunge.

I quickly throw a grin onto my face too. Rubber flaps drag across the hood, thick and slow. "I'm only just finding out about this torrid affair now?" I tease, hoping my jokey tone doesn't catch on the brambles of devastation. "What's her name?"

"It's early! I don't want to jinx it. But she's smart. And funny. And just the right amount of bitchy."

I seethe. I'm smart—I earned my associate's degree. I'm eeking out my place in LA (LA!!). And since when is "bitchy" a selling point? I remember overhearing this high school lacrosse bro off-gassing about how he was going to "fuck the bitch out" of an honor student who'd publicly rejected him at the homecoming kegger. "I love a challenge," he'd bragged, as if he had the only say in the matter. That's not who Laurel is. But what if she's got some ugly side to her I don't know about?

"Exciting," I make my mouth say. "Can't wait to meet her."

Meet, choke, whatever.

Laurel nods. "Me too. But let's see how it goes first."

Every mermaid has a sad song in her heart. Losing your great love is a requirement, the reason to strum that quiet chord of despair in each song. Cleaning fluids foam across my windshield.

This should be my big moment, here in our private tide pool, splashing salt, hope, water. But my dream has changed. I recline the driver's seat, shut my eyes to the whirring brushes. Maybe this is what a hull shearing the surface sounds like to a humpback: the whole world splicing, the disappointment of a final gasp spent on looming loss. Still, that last moment of weightlessness. Laurel and me. Free.

"What about you?" she asks.

As the car rolls into the blasting heat and water droplets reverse up the windshield, I slowly raise my seat.

"Guess now's not the time to tell you I'm madly in love with you?" I say.

Laurel stiffens, then breaks into a breezy laugh. "Oh god, no one takes it next level like you, Kansas."

I figured we'd swim through a kelp forest on our honeymoon. Not some kind of amateur hour skimming the surface with snorkels, being bogged down with air tanks on our backs, disappointing reminders that the life aquatic is temporary. I'm talking about really being there. Darting between the slippery stalks, marveling as rays of sunlight stream down on us from the surface. Living submerged.

"That's me," I force the same chuckle I'd used for Wee Witchy Wanda.

Then I remember Laurel doesn't know how to swim.

Later that afternoon, I coil onto my waterbed and stare at Jenny. Her hope. Her freedom. Dragging my desk chair to the bedroom wall, I climb up and unburden her.

"I told you," Jenny says in her sweetest voice. "No more hiding."

MOUTH

***

I stumble into the kitchen the next morning, grumpy from trying to tune out The Moaner all night. Swallowing a tablespoon of algae oil is supposed to encourage the growth of my shoulder-length frizz, and as I zombie toward the utensil drawer to measure my daily dose, I'm jarred to find The Moaner right there at the sink. Though I try to busy myself with my morning routine, I can't help but notice her strong, tan back. Angular runner's calves. Unpainted toenails, like rose quartz jeweling the desert floor. It's a body strengthened by land. Made confident by lust. As soon as she squints up at the side of the cupboard where Jenny now hangs, I know. The sun to my moon.

"Morning," she says as she turns around. "Wait, Nora?"

My blood writhes into a million ice eels when I hear her voice. Laurel. My Laurel.

"You're the annoying roommate?" she asks.

"It's my house." Her hair's twisted up in a bun and she's wearing one of Marie's tank tops. Though I've never seen her like this, I realize it's how I've always wanted to. "You're The Moaner?"

"Oh god, you could hear us?"

"It's you," I say, the words I've dreamed of telling her surging up for the wrong moment. "I can't believe it."

"Morning, babe." Marie wanders in and places a possessive hand on Laurel's lower back. As if I'm intruding on them. "Nora, meet Laurel."

"We already know each other," I say.

"Oh yeah? She hire you to do a puppet show?"

"No, we're *friends*," Laurel corrects, flaying me in the process.

"We met two years ago," I say. "My recording studio's down the street from her toy store. I can walk there."

"Funny, I met her at the toy store too. Best part about temping next door." Marie squints at the wall. "What in fuck's this thing?"

Rage makes prey of my heart. "A Jenny Haniver."

"You named it?"

"*Her*. And that's been her name for hundreds of years. There were lots of them."

Laurel moves closer, inspecting. "All posed with her hands on her hips, like she's trapped?"

"Or maybe she's something beautiful to be admired?" I offer.

Marie shanks me with some quick side-eye. "That's pretty messed up."

"Everyone deserves a little dream."

"True," she says, nuzzling Laurel's neck. "Got mine right here."

I snatch Jenny from the wall. "How could they possibly understand?" she whispers. Then we propel ourselves straight into the bathroom and unleash too much sand.

***

Two hours later, Jenny and I are surrounded by aquariums at the pet store. That low blue lighting. The gentle bubbling. Even the dried shrimp aroma: home.

"Just you and me now," I tell her.

MOUTH

"Remember who you are," she lilts as I tuck her into my coat pocket.

Back in Kansas, I lived for the county fair. Every July, in that dull pulsing summer heat, I'd put in three solid days at the carnival tossing ping pong balls, trying to win all the bagged goldfish. A lucky day would net around thirteen, and then I'd sprint to the creek behind our house and promptly set them free. Did they survive the unexpected toss into the wild? I told myself they did, but of course that wasn't the right environment for them. I still wake up in the middle of the night, panicking over their perfect O-shaped gasps and pleading, dilated eyes, my misguided grin the last thing they saw.

Which is why, when I'm upset, I beeline to the freshwater fighting fish. The ones that get their own bowls. Lightning blue, gunmetal gray. Part of me feels jealous of them, crown jewels of their own seas. But I also know what it's like to be stuck in the wrong ocean. We're all just trying to find our way to the right home.

The lids slide off easily and because my hands are slender, I can reach in without much disruption. So I do. I'm always struck by how cold their slick little bodies are. Their writhing, bendy strength. With a quick one-two swipe from the water, I do what's right and free three of them into the water-heavy zip bags lining my pockets. Then I hurry past the cashier and head outside, calmly, before Jenny, or my coat, gets soaked.

"Nora!"

Laurel's already rushing toward me, so there's no way to ignore her now. I turn to her weakly, even though the bags are wriggling. It's our first fight. I need to show up. I tighten my grip on Jenny.

"I'm really sorry," Laurel says. "Marie's crazy territorial. I think she's just jealous we met each other first."

"Why are you with someone like that?"

"You're the one that lives with her."

"With her. Not in her." I shut my eyes. I will not think of them naked together. "There are so many fish in the sea. Can you fucking go fishing somewhere else?"

"It's new. Shouldn't I give it time before I throw her back?"

"You hid something from me."

Laurel looks down. "That's the shitty part. I just wanted something to be mine for a minute, you know? To feel special. Or excited." She shakes her head. "You have your voice stuff, and what, I work in a toy shop?"

"How'd you know I'd be here anyway?"

"Where do you go when you're upset?"

I soften. I'd confided that to her months ago.

"Been sweating in the car for over an hour, waiting for you to show," she says. "You okay?"

The fish are roiling in their bags, Jenny's trying to bite my finger in protest. "I'm irritated. But I'll get over it."

"Can I make it up to you? Please?" She crosses her big brown eyes, pouting like a dumb puppy, and barks. I crack up. Gets me every time.

"Fine. When?" I ask.

"Now! C'mon, let's go have fun. A pre-birthday celebration!"

I can feel them slamming against my pockets. I purposely wore a navy blue sweatshirt under my coat to make the spillage less noticeable. "I'm not dressed for it."

MOUTH

"You look great. You don't need to change for me."

Her words unsteady me.

"I want to at least try to make it right," she says. "How about Lucky Vegetarian? My treat."

The restaurant I've been dying to try. And we're not going Dutch? That means it's technically our first date. There's an open sewer grate to the right of me. "All right. Give me a sec and then I'll follow you."

"You got it. I'm parked over there." She gestures behind her. "Drive over and honk when you're ready."

As soon as she's ensconced in her car, I hunch over the grate and dump out all three fish, praying the shallow pool at the bottom will guide them back to the ocean. But they simply bounce off a crushed water bottle and lodge in the muck, sputtering to a stop.

"That's all it takes, huh?" Jenny hisses. "Some smooth talk and you're back to your old ways?"

"It's not like that, Jenny," I say. "I made a mistake. But I love her."

"You'll have to make your choice soon."

"Why can't I have both?" I ask.

"That never works. Don't get greedy. Just stick to the goddamn plan, Nora."

***

An hour later, Laurel, Jenny, and I are seated under the jarring LED lights of Lucky Vegetarian, Jenny snug inside my pocket. Laurel and I are both powerless against eggplant in chili sauce, so we'll brave rush hour on the 10 once a month to hit up different strip mall buffets in Monterey Park. But this one, with its bright white decor, is a veritable Atlantis that I can't enjoy because my pockets are damp and I'm too nervous to speak.

"You thinking the eggplant?" Laurel asks.

"Sure."

"'Sure?'" She studies my face. "Is this going to be awkward?"

"I can't believe you're dating Marie."

"Because you can't believe I'm dating? Or you can't believe I'm dating her?"

"Both?" I say.

Laurel gets quiet. "I'm sorry."

I get quieter. "If you weren't with her?"

Laurel looks down and then I know. In that sleek restaurant booth, with a tank of bulbous orange fish as witness, the dream dissolves. Whoosh.

"I had no idea," she says.

I reel, imagining a shock of white ribs arcing from the dark seafloor. Tentacles pushing through an eye socket, lamprey writhing where baleen used to grow. A whale fall, the horror of something so grand reduced to a quiet thud.

"Do you hate me?" she asks. "Say something."

"Shittier luck than I was hoping for," I say, wiping my mouth.

She shakes her head. "I really am sorry."

Though I'm gutted, I also realize this is it. Like every mermaid before me, I've earned my heartbreak. I'm treading closer to my destiny. Jenny gives me a squeeze.

"So, tomorrow? What are you doing on your birthday?" Laurel asks.

"Heading to the beach."

"C'mon, Kansas. You've lived here for three years already! It's a half-hour from your house."

"I know, I'm ridiculous."

"You are. But that's why I love you." Her neck and chest flush red. "Wait, can I still say that? Is it too weird now?"

We've shared so much. Memories of her alcoholic mother. My social anxiety. Even the saga of her ingrown toenail (middle toe, left foot). But is that enough?

"I'm afraid of my dream coming true."

Laurel gears up as if to yell at me, but stops. Then she nods. "Well, you know I can't swim, but how about we go together?"

I smile. This is why I love her.

Our server comes by with a plate of sticky rice and mango, candle flickering. "Happy birthday!" she sings, placing it in front of me.

I shut my eyes to wish and then blow, opening them to Laurel's face, incandescent in the smoke. Jenny twists my pinkie.

Later that night, I get a text from Laurel: *Wanna do sunset tmrw? Yr actual bday! Plus fewer peeps out on a Tues. Like the whole beach is yrs. XO*

I text her immediately. *I do.*

***

All night, Jenny and I pack my treasures:

Gold-spangled seashell crown, wrapped carefully in tissue paper
- A handful of bobby pins
- Waterproof body makeup
- Eyeshadow and lipstick, also waterproof
- Clamshell bra
- Water-resistant fabric tape, two-and-a-half rolls
- Wavy blond hair extensions
- Body glitter
- Gold belly chain for added sparkle
- Jenny
- And when I unzip the garment bag, my legs tremble.

***

The next morning, packed and prepped, I head outside to sit atop the hose caddy and take in the sunrise. My birthday, the future, together now.

"It's here," Jenny says.

"I can't believe it."

"Try."

A sense of peace washes over me, and I sleep the day away.

At four o'clock that afternoon, I meet Laurel two blocks from the beach, just like we planned. Except I've also got hair extensions in and I'm pulling a suitcase behind me. Draped across my arm is my garment bag.

"Happy birthday! Jesus, what'd you bring?" she asks.

"A surprise," I say. "I want to show you something."

MOUTH

"Very mysterious, but I'll follow you."

We walk. Though the water isn't in sight yet, it's in the air: a salty lightness that slowly slips past my lips. The closer we get, the more sand blows across the sidewalk, stinging my shins. Then, when I think my knees will buckle with anticipation, it's right in front of us. Wide and welcoming. The sand, divoted with thousands of footsteps. Beyond that, sunlight chips the waves, pelicans dive bombing. I steady myself with the sidewalk handrail.

"I'm going to change," I whisper.

Laurel points to the restrooms. "Bathroom's there. I'll be here."

Inside the damp cinder block bathroom, I fill my lungs with three deep land breaths, each one gritty with the scent of salt and urine. Brackish. This bathroom must be what brackish smells like, I think, smiling. I enter a stall and get to work. Snapping. Taping. Glittering. In twenty minutes, I'm reborn.

"Happy birthday." Jenny's beaming.

I am too.

When I come out, I don't even pause at the mottled mirror above the sink. I don't need to. I shuffle along with bound steps, my feet giddy with the prospect of their new role. I pass the outdoor showering area and head straight to the volleyball nets where Laurel's stretching her quads.

She gapes. Tail. Clamshells. Me. "What's all this?"

Behind her, the indigo hour that's always felt like coming home. I inhale. "You inspired me."

Laurel's eyes move up and down my body.

"What do you think?" I ask.

Overhead, gulls squawk, just like my seashore sleep enhancers. I feel calmer, stronger.

Laurel circles me. "Can I touch it?"

"Please."

She kneels and I shake as she fans her fingers around the sequin swirls, studying the patterns, the metallic thread a fantastic find in the clearance bins at the fabric store. In her hand, the iridescence flashes. "You look beautiful."

***

The three of us shuffle across the cool sand, me barefoot and wonderous, Laurel struggling in her boots, Jenny peeking out from my suitcase. Laurel's right—at this time of day, there are only a few people out jogging after work or walking their dogs. We wait for them to pass us and once they do, I'm already standing on damp sand with a lurch behind my ribs. My hands move to my chest, trying to keep it all in.

"Here's your dream, Kansas," Laurel says, grinning. "What do you think?"

I could just sing. So I do, the lilt spouting up my throat from deep in my chest as if it too has been simply waiting for this moment. As if I need it to breathe. "It's better than I ever imagined." I open my suitcase and pull Jenny out, resting her on the suitcase facing the sea.

"Oh wow, you brought her," Laurel says.

"Home," Jenny answers.

MOUTH

I step farther out and gently lower myself to the sand. It's soft and smooth, making it easy to crawl into the ocean. Foam swells against my breastbone, the saltwater stinging my cheeks.

"Feels good, right?" Laurel calls.

"It's perfect." Every word now flowing, a song.

Though my movements are stilted because of the binding, I feel lighter than normal. Pushing myself from the sand, I roll onto my hip and marvel at my tail's cerulean brilliance under the last smolder of sunset. I stretch into the water and then flick my tail.

"Such a cool photo. Don't move." Laurel holds up her phone, trying to get a shot. But since I'm this low in the waves, I'm at their mercy as they crest over me, each swell larger than the previous one. Sky deepens into sea.

Some people are afraid of water the way they're afraid of shadows—the darkness, the shifting, the clutching undertow. But that's not being afraid of water. That's being afraid of yourself. The unknown. What you won't admit in the dark. What you'll do when your dream crests.

"Nora!" Laurel shouts.

She's knee-deep in the waves, arms beckoning me back. But the call is too loud. The waves are lifting me, welcoming me, pulling me farther.

"Be free," Jenny whispers.

With each splash, my ears dip lower into that muted world. Laurel can't swim, so she screams from the shore, her voice winging with the thermals.

Gleaming. I'm gleaming. Maybe it wasn't Laurel. Or Jenny. Maybe it was always me.

I stretch my arms wide, a Jenny unfurled. Home.

ABOUT THE AUTHOR

Growing up in the suburbs of Los Angeles during the '80s and '90s meant Kerry Donoghue spent her childhood roaming through malls. Speedwalking laps with her grandma. Trick-or-treating. Secretly kissing boys. Getting clocked while working the holiday rush. Watching where people shopped, how they dressed, and what they ate set off her fascination with consumption, a forever theme in her writing.

Her poetry and stories have appeared in *Ninth Letter*, *Painted Bride Quarterly*, *Permafrost*, *The Louisville Review*, and *The South Carolina Review*, among other journals. She also wrote *The Loudest Voice of All*, a children's book, to fundraise for an organization that educates girls about the power of voting. She earned an MFA in Writing from the University of San Francisco. You can find her in the Bay Area, eating crunchwraps by the sea, where she lives with her family and, sadly, no good malls. Get to know her at kerrydonoghue.com.

ABOUT THE PRESS

Unsolicited Press is based out of Portland, Oregon and focuses on the works of the unsung and underrepresented. As a womxn-owned, all-volunteer small publisher that doesn't worry about profits as much as championing exceptional literature, we have the privilege of partnering with authors skirting the fringes of the lit world. We've worked with emerging and award-winning authors such as Amy Shimshon-Santo, Brook Bhagat, Elisa Carlsen, Tara Stillions Whitehead, and Anne Leigh Parrish.

Learn more at unsolicitedpress.com. Find us on Instagram, X, Facebook, Pinterest, Bsky, Threads, YouTube, and LinkedIn. Unsolicited Press also writes a snarky newsletter on Substack.

www.ingramcontent.com/pod-product-compliance
Lightning Source LLC
Chambersburg PA
CBHW060023301224
19639CB00003B/102